"Becca, I like you."

He didn't care if he probably sounded li
her high school stude
had to get it out. "I li
and your kids." He st
her how much the re
the soft-serve ice crea
family they made had affected him. That would
have been *too* sappy. "I'd like to spend more time
with you."

Her shoulders sagged, and he bounced his leg in
nervous anticipation.

"Oh, Jared."

A chill went through him. *She's going to shoot me
down.* He'd had his share of brush-offs, but none
of them had felt as crushing as this would.

"I like you, too." Her lips curved in a wobbly smile.

He slid his arm along the back of the couch
behind her.

"It's too soon."

*Too soon? It had to be six or seven years since
Matt had left her.*

"I've been praying for direction in my life, about
the kids and the Nortons, about the Zoning Board
decision…" Her voice softened. "About you."

His throat clogged.

"The only answer I've gotten is 'give things time.'"

Jean C. Gordon's writing is a natural extension of her love of reading. From that day in first grade when she realized t-h-e was the word *the*, she's been reading everything she can put her hands on. Jean and her college-sweetheart husband share a 175-year-old farmhouse in Upstate New York with their daughter and her family. Their son lives nearby. Contact Jean at facebook.com/jeancgordon.author or PO Box 113, Selkirk, NY 12158.

Books by Jean C. Gordon

Love Inspired

The Donnelly Brothers

Winning the Teacher's Heart

Small-Town Sweethearts
Small-Town Dad
Small-Town Mom
Small-Town Midwife

Winning the Teacher's Heart

Jean C. Gordon

Recycling programs
for this product may
not exist in your area.

 LOVE INSPIRED BOOKS

ISBN-13: 978-0-373-87958-8

Winning the Teacher's Heart

www.Harlequin.com

Printed in U.S.A.

I will instruct you and teach you in the way you should go; I will counsel you and watch over you.
—*Psalms* 32:8

To my editor, Shana Asaro,
and my critique group BFS for helping me make
Winning the Teacher's Heart the best I could.

Chapter One

"Look out, Paradox Lake. The Donnelly brothers are back in town."

Jared Donnelly fist-bumped with his younger brothers. He didn't know about Connor and Josh, but if things worked out as he planned, he was back in the small Adirondack Mountains town for good.

"What do you think got into Old Man Miller?" Josh asked.

Jared studied a spot on the floor between him and Josh. That was a mystery to him, too. Bert Miller, their former neighbor, had unintentionally been a major factor in Jared's professional success. At least Jared thought it was unintentional, although they'd become long-distance friends of a sort over the years since Jared had left Paradox Lake.

"Not that I'm complaining," Josh said. "Without him, I'd be paying my student loans for the next two decades. But after Dad…"

Jared stiffened. Their father was one of the reasons he was back.

"You know," Josh added, "Dad gave him nothing but grief."

"Dad gave everyone nothing but grief," Connor said. "And sometimes we weren't much better."

Jared eyed his youngest brother. "You've got that right."

Connor eyed him back. "I'm not surprised Mr. Miller set up a fund for Hazardtown Community Church. He was a lifelong member. I was surprised this morning when the lawyer said that the gift was added in a recent codicil to his will, made after I was called as pastor."

Josh leaned back against the doorjamb and crossed his arms. "Connor gets money for his church. I get my student loans paid off. Jare, I think you got shortchanged. All he left you is that raw land in the Town of Schroon on the west side of Paradox Lake. No water frontage, not even a house."

"Yep, just what I need," Jared said more to himself than to his brothers.

"What?" his brothers asked in unison.

"The land's good. I may have a use for it once I get a few details worked out." He wasn't going to leave himself open to any expectations, other than his own, until he was sure his plan to build a motocross track and school— sort of a Boys & Girls Club program—was solid. "But for now, I'd better get over to Gram's. I've been in town since yesterday and haven't seen her yet."

"Right." Connor laughed. "If you don't get over there, she'll be tracking you down."

"Later," Jared said as he pushed open the screen door and stepped into the bright afternoon sun. He grabbed his helmet from the back of his customized KLR650 motorcycle, slammed it on and threw his leg over the seat. The purr of the engine when he turned the key in the ignition got his blood rushing. He gave the engine a couple of good revs and raced off on the windy mountain roads to his grandmother's house.

Fifteen minutes later, Jared slowed to take the turn off the state highway onto the side road Grandma Donnelly—Stowe—lived on. He still had trouble thinking of her as Stowe, even though she and the also-widowed Harry Stowe had married several years ago. She was on the porch waiting for him when he pulled up in front of the house.

"I heard you coming." She shooed him inside. "The black flies are still bad this year, even though June's almost over."

"That's one thing I haven't missed. But you're one I have." He gave her a big hug and kissed her cheek.

"Save your flirting for someone who's flattered by it." The pleasure radiating from her face contrasted with her words and raised a jolt of guilt in him for all the times the racing circuit had brought him near the Adirondacks, and he hadn't had the guts to make time to come to Paradox Lake.

He released a snort at the thought of what his fans would think about big, bad international motocross champion Jared Donnelly dreading a visit to his hometown.

She tilted her head. "Don't think I don't know what you've been up to. I read the magazines."

Jared cringed. He didn't know if he should be disturbed or flattered that she followed him in the media. "Aw, Gram, you don't believe all that drivel."

"No." She smiled. "I know you better than that. Join me for lunch? Harry's at one of his rental houses getting an estimate on some repairs. He said he'd get lunch at the diner in Schroon Lake so we'd have time for a nice visit."

"Sounds good." Considering her husband Harry's penchant for talking and knowing everyone from his years as a teacher and principal at Schroon Lake Central High

School, he and Gram probably would have all afternoon for visiting.

"Come on in the kitchen. I figured you'd stop over after you and your brothers got back from the lawyer's. I have iced tea all made. I just need to put some sandwiches together."

A brief rap, followed by a cheery "hello" and the creak of the screen door opening made Jared and his grandmother turn around in the kitchen doorway.

His chest tightened so he could barely draw a breath. Becca Morgan—Norton—stood in his grandmother's living room looking as pretty and as untouchable to him as she had in high school.

Becca looked Jared over from his tousled chestnut hair to his strong square jaw and muscular physique. He was taller and more filled out than he'd been in high school when she used to secretly watch him—watch him with the knowledge that despite Schroon Lake High School's small student body, he didn't seem to know she even existed. Her cheeks pinked when her stare met his.

"Oh." She stopped midstep. "I didn't know you had company. I brought the dishwasher detergent you asked me to pick up for you in Ticonderoga."

"Thanks again. I don't know why the grocery store in Schroon Lake quit carrying it." Edna Stowe bustled into the living room and took the bag from Becca.

"Mom!" Becca's son, Brendon, lined up beside her, followed by his sister, Ariana. "That's the guy in my motorcycle magazine Grandpa Norton bought me."

She cleared her throat. "Yes, that's Jared Donnelly."

"Right here at Mrs. Stowe's house?"

Edna laughed. "Yes, Brendon. Jared is my grandson. Jared, this is Becca's son, Brendon, and his sister, Ari."

At the mention of her name, Ari wrapped her arms around Becca's leg and peered across the room at Jared, sort of like Becca had at school when she'd known Jared wasn't looking. But that was a long time ago in another life.

"Mr...Mr. Donnelly. If I get my motocross magazine, will you sign it next to your picture?"

"Sure." Jared hooked his thumbs in his jeans pockets.

"It's in the car. I'll go get it." The boy raced out.

"And I'm going to go back in the kitchen and finish making our lunch. Do you and the kids want to join us?"

"No, thanks. I treated them to fast food after we finished shopping."

Jared moved out of the doorway to let his grandmother through and sauntered over to Becca. "Your son's a motocross fan?"

"Since last month when his grandfather bought him a magazine at the chain pharmacy in Ticonderoga."

"Sheriff Norton." Jared's tone was flat.

"Former sheriff. He and my mother-in-law—ex-mother-in-law—are retired and thinking about moving to Florida. The North Country winters are getting to them." Becca rubbed Ari's shoulder. Why was she running on about Matt's parents? What would Jared care if they were moving to Florida or to the moon?

"Winter is something I'm going to have to get used to again," he said.

Becca's mouth went dry. That sounded as if Jared intended to stay in Paradox Lake for a while. Not that she cared. She'd barely known Jared before he'd left here as a teen. She certainly didn't know the man who'd filled the doorway when she'd first arrived. She looked over her shoulder at the creak of the door opening.

"Here it is. I got it." Brendon waved his magazine at

her as he raced across the room. "And Mom's pen from the car."

"Let's see what you have there," Jared said.

Her heart warmed when he squatted down to her son's level. She didn't know or care whether the interest on his face was real or feigned. Brendon's father gave him so little of the quality attention her son needed and wanted. Jared's attention would make her son's day.

"That's one of my favorite magazines. The writers stick to the important stuff, the real motocross news."

The edge she caught in his voice made her think of a derogatory comment the kids' grandfather had made about Jared's offtrack life being splashed on the front of another magazine he'd seen at the store.

Brendon leafed through the magazine. "Here." The nine-year-old tapped the page several time. "This is you."

"So it is," Jared agreed with a smile.

"Sign here on your motorcycle." Brendon gave the page another stab.

Jared signed with a flourish, hamming it up for her son's benefit.

"Mommy!" Ari pulled her attention from Jared and Brendon still bent over the magazine, Jared's dark hair a sharp contrast to her son's fair hair. "Can I go get my storybook from the car so the man can sign it, too?"

"The man is Mr. Donnelly."

"Jared." He raised his head, his deep blue eyes challenging her to object.

"Can I have Mr. Donnelly sign my book?"

Good girl. She could always count on Ari to do as she was told. Becca caught the sparkle in Jared's eyes. *Maybe too much so.* She reminded Becca so much of herself at Ari's age when her parents had separated temporarily after their third child had been stillborn. The uncertain feelings, wanting to do everything right so Daddy wouldn't leave, too, and Mommy would come back.

Jared rose and flexed his knees. "You don't want me scribbling in your book."

Ari's face crinkled.

"I have a better idea. You and your mommy go get the book and I'll read it to you. I used to read to my little brother all the time when our mom worked nights," Jared added as if to explain his offer.

Becca swallowed the protest she'd been about to make about keeping him and his grandmother from their lunch. She hadn't known his mother worked nights, only the town gossip about his father's partying. Jared was the oldest. He must have watched his brothers for her.

"You two go and get the book," Jared said. "I'll tell Gram to hold lunch for a few minutes."

"Thanks," Becca mouthed over Ari's head before they walked out to the car.

Jared and Brendon were on the couch looking at the motocross magazine when they returned. Jared patted the seat beside him and Ari looked up at her for an okay. Her chest tightened as she nodded. Ari scrambled over and plopped her book on top of the magazine.

Becca hung back, feeling as out of place as she had in high school when she hadn't been insulated by her small circle of friends. She shook it off. She'd been a cheerleader, an honor student, part of the popular group at school. She'd worked hard to never show how shy she really was. Now, she was a tenured high school teacher, mother, homeowner. What was it about Jared Donnelly that put her off-kilter?

"Becca." Mrs. Stowe motioned her from the kitchen doorway. "Come out to the garden with me while Jared's reading. I planted far too much lettuce and spinach as usual. Pick some to take home with you." The older woman handed her a basket in the back hall behind the kitchen and led the way to the large garden.

"Take as much as you want. Harry is tired of salads. My kids have their own gardens, and my only grandkids who are still around here are Jared's brothers. They aren't vegetable fans. I hate to see good food go to waste."

"Since you put it that way." Becca filled the basket.

When they got back inside, Jared was just closing the book.

"Mommy, Mr. ...*Jared*—" Ari said, looking up at him with a sheen in her eyes that could only be described as adoration "—read the story twice because you were taking so long. But that's okay. It's a good story and he's a good reader."

Brendon rolled his eyes and the three adults laughed.

"Get your book and thank Mr. Donnelly. We need to get going so he and Mrs. Stowe can have their lunch."

"Okay. Thanks for reading my story."

"Yeah, thanks." Brendon tilted his rolled magazine toward Jared.

"You're both welcome." Jared stood and walked out to the porch with them.

The kids waved to him as she turned the car around, and she sensed his gaze on her as she pulled to the end of the driveway. She glanced back and he waved. Jared Donnelly had finally noticed her—at the absolutely worst time possible.

Jared took his time joining his grandmother in the kitchen. Becca's kids had seemed to like him. But they were young and full of hero worship. He wasn't anyone's hero. He was simply very good at motocross racing, something he was going to use to help his hometown and show everyone he and his brothers weren't cut from the same cloth as their father.

"Everything's ready," his grandmother said as he sat at the kitchen table across from her.

He picked up his sandwich.

"Would you say grace?"

"Sure." He placed the sandwich back on the plate and blessed their food. "I got out of the practice on the circuit," he apologized. "Even with the pit pastors as a reminder."

"Yes, I read the article on Team Faith you emailed me. I'm glad you had the fellowship of other Christians, especially with what you went through after your friend was killed."

"I knew you would be." His out-of-control actions following his best friend and mentor's death in a crash had made Jared wonder if he had more of his father in him than he cared to admit.

"And I knew not to believe what I saw in the grocery store scandal sheets, even—or I should say, especially— when some people around here ate those stories up."

"What could you expect given how Dad was?" Jared's fingers tightened around his glass of tea. He wasn't going to have an easy time changing people's minds about him. Bert Miller's bequest would be a big help, though. For whatever reason, Bert had had faith in him when no one except his mother and grandmother had. And sometimes he wasn't so sure about his mother. Not that he could blame her.

"Gram, you and Mom are good people, and so was Grandpa. I've always wondered how Dad went so wrong."

She shook her head. "I don't know. He was already grown when I took the teaching job at Schroon Lake and met your grandfather. But we don't want to talk about your father."

His father was a subject Jared usually avoided, but, surprisingly, he did want to talk about him now. He wouldn't press Gram, though, if she didn't want to.

"You sure hit it off with Becca's kids," she said.

He shrugged and took a big bite of his sandwich.

"I've always liked Becca Norton," she said.

He swallowed the bite. So had he. From afar.

"Weren't you in the same grade?

"No, she was a year ahead of me." One more thing that had put her out of his reach. Jared pictured Becca as she'd looked the first time he'd seen her, at the beginning of his freshman year. Her waist-length hair. Her bright friendly smile. Her hair was shorter now, but the smile was the same.

"That's right," his grandmother said. "She came to Schroon Lake Central from Lakeside Christian Academy the year Harry became principal." Her eyes went soft when she mentioned her husband of three years.

Jared reached for his tea. With a kindergarten-through-twelfth-grade student body of less than three hundred, any new student at Schroon Lake Central School stuck out. But Becca had even more so—at least for him. He'd told his buddy he'd be taking her to the homecoming dance. His friend's derisive laugh had made him more determined—until his father had gone and ruined everything before he'd even gotten to meet her. He gulped the rest of his drink.

"Becca and I taught together for a couple of years before I retired. I think both Josh and Connor had her for history at least one year. Which reminds me. Do you know if Connor has made up his mind yet? I think Becca would be perfect."

Connor and Becca? He gripped the empty glass. "Isn't he a little young for her?"

His grandmother's lips twitched. "I don't see what Connor's age has to do with hiring Becca to be the substitute head teacher at The Kids' Place, the church daycare center, for the summer. She could use the money."

"Nothing." He studied a small chip in his sandwich plate, most likely courtesy of him or one of his brothers or cousins. Gram had been feeding them sandwiches on the same plates since they were kids. "My mind was elsewhere."

The twitch turned into a knowing smile. Except Gram didn't really know anything about it. Becca Norton was an adolescent dream he had no intention of pursuing as an adult. They had been too different then and were too different now.

"Would you like a piece of strawberry-rhubarb pie?" She stood and turned to the counter behind her chair. "I baked one this morning. I remember it was always your favorite."

Jared pursed his lips, irritated that Gram's smile bothered him.

"It's not that big of a decision," she said making as if to place the pie back on the counter.

"Sorry, Gram. I'd love a piece of your pie." He lifted his empty plate toward her, and she cut and placed a large slice on it.

"Something's bothering you." It was a statement, not a question.

"I'm fine." He bit into a forkful of pie. "This is great."

"You haven't said anything about what the lawyer said this morning. I assume it was about Bert Miller's will."

Jared chewed the pie, savoring the combination of sweet and tart. "He left Connor a trust for the church, paid off Josh's student loans and gave me that land he owned west of the lake."

His grandmother's eyes widened. "Did you know?"

"Not about Josh and Connor."

"But about the land?" she pressed.

He tapped his fork on the side of the plate before setting it down. "He sent me a letter a couple of months ago."

"Oh."

"He used to do that, send me a letter every so often."

Gram tilted her head and studied him. "Bert always did like you boys." She hesitated as if weighing her next words. "Said you were the sons he never had."

"He was with Dad that night…you know…he told me in one of his letters."

"I know."

Jared jerked his head up. From what Bert had said in his letter, he'd gotten the idea that fact wasn't common knowledge.

"Your father told your grandfather one night when he'd been drinking."

Jared stifled a snort. That could have been about any night.

"Your grandfather told me your dad and Bert had been best friends since kindergarten. Until then."

Gram was the only grandmother he remembered. But she hadn't married his widowed grandfather until after Jared had been born. She'd always been able to talk about Dad with a lot more detachment than he or either of his brothers could.

He pushed away from the table. "I should get going." Now that Gram wanted to talk about Dad, Jared wasn't sure he did anymore.

"JJ." His grandmother reached across the table and touched his hand.

He pulled away from her touch at the use of his child-hood nickname, short for Jared Junior. "Don't call me that. Please." He softened his tone.

"You're not your father."

Jared released his pent up breath. "I know, but I did enough stupid things before I left Paradox Lake, and some after, to make people think I am."

"Honey, you weren't the first or the last teenager in Paradox Lake to be stopped driving while impaired."

"I'm the only son of the town drunk who was, after knocking over the Sheriff's mailbox and running down his front fence."

"You paid back Sheriff Norton for all the damages to his property."

"After which he strongly recommended I take myself elsewhere as soon as I finished high school."

"He was harsher on you than he might have been on someone else. There was bad blood between him and your father. But now you're back. And I, for one, am glad you are."

"Yep, I'm back." And there wasn't anyone or anything that could make him leave again. At least not before he cleaned up the Donnelly family name and made amends to his brothers for bailing on them and his mother.

Becca kept an eye on Brendon and Ari from the kitchen window that overlooked the backyard as she put away the groceries she'd picked up in Ticonderoga. Her son was racing his bike around Ari and the jungle gym her father had built for them before he and her mother had moved to North Carolina. Probably pretending he was Jared. He and motocross racing were all Brendon had talked about on the drive home from Edna Stowe's house.

She closed the cupboard and walked out to the deck

to call the kids in to get their things ready to go to their other grandparents' for the night.

"Hey, Mom, watch." Brendon rode his bike up a small rise behind the jungle gym and sped down, yanking on the bike's handle bars and doing a wheelie for several feet across the yard. She stifled a screech as he circled around and laid the bike down on the grass in front of the deck steps.

"What do you think?" He beamed.

What she thought was she was likely to be completely gray by the time she was thirty-five. "Impressive," she said.

"Do you think if I asked Dad, he would buy me a dirt bike for my birthday?"

Becca closed her eyes and breathed in and out. If her ex-husband knew how much that thought terrorized her, he probably would and count the cost as child support. She'd never shared it with Matt, but her parents had instilled a fear of motorcycles in her when she was a child after a close friend of theirs had died in a bike accident.

"I think you should wait a few more years on that one." Brendon was only nine going on ten.

"Aw, Jared could teach me how to ride. The story in the magazine said that he's going to start a school to teach kids like me how to race motocross, with a real motocross racetrack and everything."

"I don't think he's building his racetrack here." Jared Donnelly hadn't been back to Paradox Lake for more than an occasional short visit since he'd left fifteen years ago. Even if he were in town for an extended visit, she doubted he'd build his motocross school here in the North Country where he could only operate it part of the year.

The disappointment on Brendon's face made her chest tighten. He was just a little boy, even though he often seemed older because of his self-appointed role as the man of the family since her ex had left them.

She draped her arm over his shoulder, expecting him to duck out of her loose embrace, and her heart warmed when he didn't. "You and Ari need to get ready to go to Grandma and Grandpa's. They'll be here soon to pick you guys up for the pizza movie night at church. Is Ian going?"

"Yeah." Brendon shrugged away. "His parents would probably let him get a dirt bike."

Back to that. Becca was pretty certain her son's best friend's parents would no more buy Ian a dirt bike than she'd let Brendon have one. "Go on and get your sleepover stuff ready. I'll be right in with Ari."

Brendon stomped off.

"Ari, we need to pack your things for Grandma's."

"Okay, Mom." She jumped off the swing and skipped up the stairs to the deck.

A few minutes later, Becca watched her former in-laws and her kids drive away. Fortunately, they'd been running late, so she hadn't had to talk with them much beyond finding out when they'd be bringing the kids back tomorrow. She walked to the kitchen, poured a glass of ice tea and took a carton of yogurt from the refrigerator before going back out onto the deck. Brendon had left his magazine on the umbrella table. She sat on the matching chair and leafed through the magazine to a page with a picture of Jared standing beside a racing bike with his helmet tucked under his arm. His hair was tousled as if he'd just taken off the helmet, and he oozed masculine bravado. In the accompanying article, Jared talked about starting a motocross school for kids, particularly under-privileged and fatherless kids.

She closed the publication and placed it on the table.

Brendon wasn't underprivileged, but she often felt he was growing up fatherless. She'd taken her wedding vows seriously. Tried and prayed so hard to keep her marriage together, and, despite knowing better, couldn't shake the final remnants of failure that she hadn't been able to. As if to block out the pain, her mind went to Ari and Brendon sitting on either side of Jared on his grandmother's couch looking at Ari's storybook. A perfect family picture. Something beyond her reach. Obviously, she wasn't cut out for marriage if she couldn't make a go of it with someone she'd grown up with and had known as well as Matt. Or thought she'd known.

The picture of Jared with her kids popped back into her head. She had no idea why her mind was flitting from him to marriage and back to him. Regardless of what he'd said at his grandmother's about getting used to Adirondack winters again, she couldn't imagine he was back to stay. What attraction, besides his family, could Paradox Lake hold for someone who'd traveled all around the world?

Becca pushed Jared and her failed marriage out of her head. Looking past her yard beyond her property to the meadow and woods that Bert Miller had owned, she wondered what would become of the acreage. Her ex-mother-in-law had been sure Bert would leave it to her, his only relative. But that didn't seem to be the case. She placed her elbows on the table and rested her chin on her entwined fingers. Last year, she and the two other families on Conifer Road had heard Bert was considering selling it to a resort syndicate that was vying for one of the gambling casino licenses New York State had up for grabs at the time. They'd banded together in an informal homeowners association, ready to oppose that project or any other undesirable one that might endanger the quality of life they wanted for their families.

She hoped it wouldn't come to anything like that. Recently, hanging on to her property had become enough of a fight for her. She didn't need another one. Raising two kids and paying the mortgage on the *dream* house she and her ex-husband had built was tough on a teacher's salary, especially a teacher's salary at a small school such as Schroon Lake. She nudged a stone under the table with her toe. Getting the job she'd applied for running The Kids' Place at church for the summer would really help. Disappointment welled inside her. She'd thought she would have heard back by now. The only other jobs available were in the tourist trade and wouldn't pay enough for her to make any money once she'd paid for day care. Unless she asked her ex-mother-in-law to watch them, which she wasn't about to do. Ari and Brendon could come with her to The Kids' Place. She kicked the stone and watched it arch up and hit the deck rail before landing on the grass several feet away.

She rose to go inside. Why did she always have to second-guess herself and overthink everything? Why couldn't she simply accept God's plan for her? Her mind flashed back once more to Jared reading to her kids and she halted midstep. *That* couldn't possibly be what He had in mind for her.

Chapter Two

The summer breeze ruffled Becca's hair. She pushed a stray strand behind her ear and adjusted her seat on a boulder left courtesy of the advance or retreat of a prehistoric glacier. Science had never been her subject. A motion to her left caught her attention. Someone, a man, was walking toward her. She tensed. There was no place for her to go. This wasn't even her property. She looked at her house in the distance on the other side of the meadow.

"Becca?" The figure called.

She shielded her eyes from the late-morning sun. *Jared.* His smooth, cocky gait was a dead giveaway if she hadn't recognized his voice. "Hi," she called back with a wave.

"What brings you out here?" he asked when he reached her.

"I could ask you the same." She smiled. "I often walk the meadow. That's my house over there." She pointed to the colonial on a rise framed by tall pines.

"And you're sitting on my rock." He grinned back.

"Your rock?"

"Yep, Bert Miller left me this property. So, we're neighbors."

"Oh." She dropped her gaze. That sounded brilliant. He looked around behind her. "No kids?"

"They stayed overnight with their grandparents, Matt's parents, last night. Under our custody agreement, Matt's supposed to have them every other weekend. But he's in Connecticut and works a lot of weekends. Ken and Debbie often take his time." *Too often.* She clamped her hand over her mouth. Why was she running on about the Nortons again, making excuses for the kids' father? Matt had made enough excuses before and after he'd left them. She didn't need to make more for him.

Jared's mouth tightened, then relaxed. "Nice day. I'd almost forgotten what mountain summers are like."

"So, how long are you staying? Your grandmother's really been looking forward to your visit." She pushed away from the boulder and stood.

"Indefinitely. I guess Gram didn't tell you I'm moving here."

"Here?" She motioned toward the meadow. Jared Donnelly was going to be her neighbor? Brendon would be thrilled. Her heart tripped as if to deny her first thought that having Jared so close wouldn't be a good idea.

"Not right here. I have other plans for this property. For now, I'm staying with Connor."

The guarded look in his eyes stopped her from asking about his plans. She checked her watch. "I'd better get back to the house. The Nortons will be bringing the kids home soon." *And if I'm not there, it'll be one more strike against me in their virtual book of reasons I'm not a good mother.*

"I'll walk back with you. I've seen all I need to see, and I'm going that direction anyway. I parked my bike in the gravel pull-in up the road from your house."

"That would be a pretty spot to build a house." What

was with her? One minute she was concerned about Jared owning the property adjacent to hers. The next she sounded as if she was encouraging him to build a house there.

"True." He fell into step with her.

After a few yards of uncomfortable silence, she asked. "Have you really retired from motocross? That's what Brendon's magazine said."

"You read the feature about me."

"Some of it," she admitted. He grinned and her stomach fluttered. She should have had more for breakfast than toast and coffee.

"Yep, at thirty-three I'm the old man of the circuit, and I thought it was best to go out while I'm still at the top. If you asked some of my rivals, they'd say about time. Mom and Gram say past time."

Becca nodded. "I know how worried your grandmother was about you when you had that accident last year."

He shrugged. "Part of the business. It wasn't that bad. I'd had worse. But I'm ready to move on and give some of the younger guys a shot at the winner's circle."

From someone else, Jared's words would have sounded boastful. And she knew about boastful from being married to Matt Norton. But from Jared they sounded matter-of-fact.

"It's going to be quite a change for you, going from the life of a national motocross champion to living back here in Paradox Lake."

"Not so much as you might think. The circuit isn't all glitter and parties like the magazines make it look. I will miss the rush of crossing the finish line. But I have something in mind to do that could be even more satisfying. I'd like to—"

"Oh, no!" Becca interrupted him as they crested the rise. He stopped.

"Sorry," she said. "That's the Nortons' car." Her heart pounded as she pointed toward the highway. "I've got to be at the house before they are."

She had enough stress in her life with her car on its last legs and no summer job in sight. She didn't need the Nortons complaining about her not being there for the kids to anyone who would listen and talking Matt into taking her to Family Court again for more visitation time—at the expense of less child support. Time the kids most likely would end up spending with their grandparents, not their father. Thankfully, she'd put on her athletic shoes this morning rather than a pair of sandals.

She took off with Jared easily keeping up with her. They reached Becca's backyard before the Nortons pulled into her driveway. She bent over to catch her breath. When she straightened, Jared was pressing buttons on his cell phone.

"Forty-five seconds flat," he said.

Despite her agitation, she laughed. "You did not time me."

"No, but you worked up some speed there. I don't remember you running track."

She shook the tingle from her hands. Jared remembered what sports she'd played in high school. "I didn't take up running until I had Brendon and Ari." *And ex-in-laws who seem to keep tabs on my every move when the kids are involved.*

"I'm sure the two of them keep you hopping, and I don't just mean physically."

"You're right there. Keeping ahead of them mentally is as much of a race as chasing them around when they were toddlers."

The Nortons' car pulled into the driveway as she and Jared rounded the corner of the house. The Sheriff—she always thought of her ex-father-in-law that way, rather than by his first name—threw open his door and got out. His wife, Debbie, took her time, turning to say something to Brendon and Ari in the backseat before stepping out and opening their door.

"Mommy!" Ari propelled herself out of the car. "We saw *The Lego Movie* last night and had popcorn and soda and everything."

"I thought we might see you there," Debbie said with obvious disapproval. "Emily Stacey and her brother, Neal, brought their families."

She would not let her ex-mother-in-law make her feel guilty for having an evening to herself. "I didn't want to intrude on your time with the kids," Becca said, very aware of Jared standing behind her.

"Jared, Mom didn't say you were going to come over today." The boy looked around. "Did you ride your bike? Remember, you said you'd take me for a ride if it was okay with Mom."

Becca closed her eyes. *Not the thing to say.* The spill-over from the annual Americade motorcycle rally in Lake George had not endeared bikers to the Sheriff. That he'd bought Brendon the motocross magazine only attested to her son's power of persuasion.

"Grandpa." Brendon grabbed the older man's hand and pulled him toward her and Jared. "This is Jared, the guy in my magazine. I told you he was at Mrs. Stowe's."

Ken Norton glared at Jared. "Donnelly, I heard you were back."

Tension radiated from Jared.

"Sheriff."

"Interesting to run into you here at my daughter-in-law's this *morning*." Ken looked from Jared to her and back. "Where's your vehicle? Hidden out back so the neighbors can't see it?"

Becca gasped. She couldn't believe Ken would think such a thing, let alone say it. She sensed, rather than saw, Jared move to her defense and shook her head.

Dear Lord, she prayed silently. *Please help me. I don't have the fortitude for this.*

It took every ounce of strength Jared had not to punch the smirk off Sheriff Norton's face. *The jerk.* Jared didn't know what had gone on between Becca and Matt Norton beyond hearing that Matt had left Becca for another woman. Nor did he know what kind of woman Becca was now, except that his grandmother thought highly of her. None of it was his business. But he wasn't going to stand here and let the man insult Becca like that in front of her children, even if they were too young to get their grandfather's implied meaning.

Jared fisted and unfisted his hands—twice. "My motorcycle is up the road in the pull-in." He ground out each word. "I drove over this morning to walk my new property."

"You didn't come to read me another story?" Ari asked. "You said yesterday that you would sometime."

"No, sweetie," Becca said. "Mr. Donnelly didn't come to read to you today."

Jared admired how calm and collected Becca was. He smiled down at the little girl. "But I will another time. I promise."

The Nortons exchanged a glance.

Let them think what they liked. Jared stepped forward and positioned himself to one side of Becca, between her and the Nortons. *As long as their evil thoughts didn't go beyond the two of them.*

"Brendon, take Ari in, and you two put away your overnight things. Yesterday's clothes can go in the clothes hamper. I'll be in in a minute."

"Jared, too?" Brendon looked at him expectantly.

"No, Mr. Donnelly won't be coming in."

Becca's tone brooked no argument from Brendon or him. But Becca wasn't the person he itched to argue with.

"When you finish, you can each have one of the brownies I made this morning. They're on the counter." She softened her tone.

"That may not be a good idea," their grandmother said. "I made them chocolate chip pancakes with whipped cream for breakfast. You don't want them to have too much sugar."

To Jared, it sounded as though that ship had already sailed.

The kids looked from their grandmother to their mother.

"It's okay," Becca said. "You can have a brownie. But only one each."

Debbie Norton pasted a smile over the frown that creased her face and held out her arms. "Give Grandma a kiss goodbye."

The kids took their time walking over to her. They each pecked her cheek.

"Come on, Ari," Brendon said. "Let's go get our brownie."

"Clothes first," Becca reminded them.

"Yeah, clothes first. Bye, Jared."

"Bye," his sister echoed.

"See you guys."

Brendon stopped. "Tomorrow? Maybe you could give me a bike ride?"

"And read me another story," Ari said. "You could come to Sunday school tomorrow and read the story. I'm sure Mrs. Stacey wouldn't mind."

Jared pictured himself surrounded by a class of five-year-olds with only his former classmate Emily "Jinx" Hazard Stacey as his backup defense and suppressed a shudder.

"Inside," Becca said, rescuing him from the thought.

"Okay! Come on Ari," Brendon said. The two trooped off to the house.

Once they were out of hearing range, Jared faced Sheriff Norton and waited for Becca to say something about his insinuations. She didn't. Jared looked from the Sheriff to her, and she dropped her gaze.

"So, Donnelly," the Sheriff said before Jared could mentally fit together even one piece of the puzzle that was Becca. "I take it Bert carried through with his foolish idea of penance."

"I don't know what you mean."

Becca put an extra step between them, the icy edge of his reply seeming to have caught her more than his intended target.

The Sheriff transferred his glare from Jared to her. "Shouldn't you be in the house with the kids?"

"No, I'm sure they're fine."

Jared raised his head to the sky. Now Becca decided to stand her ground, over his business, rather than standing up for herself.

Ken dismissed her with a shake of his head and drilled his gaze into Jared's. "Bert ignored his family and went ahead and left you this property. I suppose he gave your brothers something, too."

"Yes, he gave me the acreage here. You'll have to check the county records for any other information you feel you need to know."

Ken pursed his lips. "Hope you guys enjoy your blood money." He jerked his head toward his car and his wife started walking toward it.

She stopped at the door and turned to Becca. "See you at church tomorrow." She climbed in the car and her husband gunned the engine and roared out of the driveway.

"She almost makes me want to skip service," Becca said. "But your brother gives some of the most thought-provoking sermons. I'd hate to miss one just to spite them."

Becca's enthusiasm for his brother brought back a little of the sting he'd felt yesterday when his grandmother's words had made him think Connor was interested in Becca. He shook it off. "I wouldn't waste perfectly good spite on Sheriff Norton. What's with him anyway?"

Becca hesitated. "I…we…you mean, about the land."

"Yeah." As much as he'd wanted to light into Ken for what he'd said to Becca, he had no desire to get involved in whatever was between her and her ex-in-laws.

"Debbie is, was, Bert's cousin, his only living relative. From what she said to me when he was first diagnosed, she'd expected to inherit everything. She and Ken were looking at it as a nice addition to their retirement assets."

She shivered in the warm breeze and he checked himself from putting his arm around her shoulder.

"Debbie made a big show of going to visit him when he went into hospice. I don't know that she talked to him three times a year before that."

"She didn't get his house, either."

"Pardon?"

"Bert didn't leave her his house either. He left that

to one of the county home health aides he particularly liked. She told us at the reading of the will that when she told Bert her rent had gone up and she was going to have to move, he'd said he'd leave her his house. She never dreamed he'd been serious. Everything else went to the hospice organization and us."

She touched her fingertip to her lips. "Strange. I had no idea you were close to him."

"We weren't. I worked for him some when I was a teenager."

"Not to pry, but I'm curious about what Ken meant about blood money."

"You caught that, too. I don't know."

"As a friend—" Jared was so focused on Becca considering him a friend that he almost missed the rest "—let me tell you that you don't want to do anything to make an enemy out of Sheriff Norton, or Debbie, for that matter."

Too late for that. It appeared he'd already made it back on the Sheriff's enemy list without even trying. He looked at her solemn face. From her warning, at least Becca seemed to be on his side.

Jared hung up from the call with his financial adviser and dropped his cell phone next to him on the futon. Things were coming together. The contingent financing approval he'd applied for before returning to Paradox Lake had gone through. He glanced around the spare room Connor was letting him use. A basic twentysomething male room, from the garage-sale dresser to the footlocker at the end of the futon. Grandpa Donnelly's antique polished-wood rolltop desk stuck out like a bicycle in a motocross race. Because Jared had loved the desk as a kid, loved rolling it shut and open, Grandma Donnelly had given it to him for his twentieth birthday and first major motocross win. He'd retrieved it from Gram's the day after he'd run into Becca and the Nortons.

He locked his fingers behind his head and leaned back into the lumpy cushions. He should start thinking about a permanent residence. *Permanent.* He liked the sound of that. Becca was right that the land fronting the road by the pull-in would make a nice house lot. But after nearly fifteen years on the circuit living, breathing, sleeping work, he wanted to put some space between his home and his work. Not that he'd mind having Becca as a neighbor. He crossed his legs at his ankles and jiggled his foot. He hoped she and the other two residents of Conifer Road wouldn't mind having him building his track and racing school there. Jared was expecting some opposition, but he was prepared.

"Hey, big brother." Connor appeared in the doorway. "I figured I'd find you here goofing off."

"This from a man who works for an hour one day a week?"

"Right."

Jared swung off the futon. "What's up?"

"I'm going for a swim down at the Camp Sonrise beach, one of the perks of having the Hazard family as parishioners. Want to come?"

"Sure. Give me a minute to change."

"I'll be out front."

Jared bounded down the steps two minutes later. "We can take my bike."

"No, let's jog down to the lake. I need as much physical activity as possible to work off my morning."

Jared studied his brother. "You had office hours this morning. Bad news?"

Connor waved him off. "No. The toddler room teacher

at The Kids' Place called in sick. Becca had trouble finding a substitute."

"I take that to mean you hired Becca." That would explain why he hadn't seen her car in her driveway either of the times he'd been back over to his property.

"Yeah. Didn't I tell you?" Connor picked up his pace. "Becca had me cover with the teacher's aide until she could find someone else."

"Gram said something about your dragging your feet about hiring her."

"Hey, it wasn't me. It was the day-care board."

"They gave you a hard time? What could they have against Becca?" What could anyone have against her?

"Debbie Norton is on the board. She got some of the other members questioning whether we wanted to hire a divorcée. After Matt was the one who abandoned Becca and the kids for another woman *and* initiated the divorce."

Jared pounded ahead, hitting the road so hard it sent a bolt of pain up the shin he'd broken in his accident last year.

"Sanity prevailed. We didn't have anyone else who was as qualified as Becca, and she's only filling in until the head teacher we hired for the fall can start." Connor pulled ahead. "Since when have you been interested in small-town, social-political gossip?"

Jared switched gears into a full run. Forget the pain. He couldn't believe how cruel and meddlesome Becca's ex-in-laws were to her. "Since you became the purveyor of such information."

Connor shrugged and matched Jared's speed. "It comes with the territory, and I shouldn't have shared that, even with you. All I wanted was some sympathy for having to spend two hours with a room full of two-year-olds. I certainly didn't get any from the women."

"That tough?" The men hit the beach with Jared a stride ahead and then slowed to a trot.

"That tough. Remind me of this morning if I ever get any ideas of having kids of my own."

"Becca's kids seem okay," Jared said without thinking. "But you're right. Us Donnelly men are not cut out to be parents." He stopped at the camp dock, dropped the towel he'd hung around his neck and pulled off his T-shirt.

Connor followed suit. "So, that's the way it is. Becca Norton."

Jared answered his brother by diving into the lake. "Whoa!" he shouted when he surfaced.

"Yeah, bro, I meant to tell you. With the below-normal temperatures we've had at night this month, the lake's cold."

"No, it's great. Just what I needed." *To cool off my reaction to your too-close taunt, little brother.*

Connor shot off the dock with a cannonball.

"Way to go, Pastor Connor. That was a good one."

Jared shook off the water Connor had splashed in his face. A small mob of kids was invading the beach, led by several women, including Becca and Jinx Hazard Stacey. "Look out, Conn. They're coming for you."

Connor paddled over to the dock ladder. "No, that's the third- through sixth-grade kids," he said over his shoulder. "They're people. Nothing like the little darlings I got to experience down and dirty this morning."

Jared followed him up the ladder and picked up his towel. "You were two once. I remember you being two. Mom used to make me watch you in the backyard so she could get stuff done in the house."

"I was one kid. There was a whole herd of them at day care."

"Sure." Jared toweled his hair dry.

"So, this is where you ran off to," Becca said.

Jared peered out from under the towel to see her and Jinx stepping onto the dock.

"You've got that right." Connor tossed his towel over his shoulder and gave an exaggerated shudder.

"You should have seen Connor," Becca said. "I wish I'd had my phone with me to catch his look of pure terror when I walked him into the room after he'd agreed to help the teacher's aide."

"I heard all about it." Jared dried off quickly and pulled on his T-shirt, feeling inexplicably self-conscious in front of Becca and Jinx without it.

"Hey, Donnelly, it's okay. We've seen men at the beach before," Jinx teased.

Strange, the sun wasn't that intense that his cheeks should feel so warm. "Jinx Hazard. How have you been?"

"Emily Stacey now. And I've been good."

"I know, Mom and Gram have kept me up to date."

Becca pushed her hair behind her ears and looked from him to Jinx, seemingly confused by their banter. "I hadn't realized you two were friends."

They weren't really. They'd simply shared the affinity of both being students on the fringe of their high school's cliques and an ambition to get out of Paradox Lake as soon as they'd graduated. He doubted Becca and her popular crowd had ever noticed either of them.

"I could say the same about you two."

"When Emily returned to Paradox Lake to stay with her niece a few years ago, we connected and found we had a lot in common."

Becca caught and held his gaze until he contemplated another dive into the lake.

"Jared." Brendon and another boy about his size clambered onto the dock, breaking the connection. A connection that probably existed only in his wishful mind.

"Tell Ian that you *are* the guy in my magazine. He doesn't believe me."

"I am."

Brendon's red-haired friend scrutinized him. "You sort of look like the picture."

"That's your motorcycle in Pastor Connor's driveway. Right, Jared?"

"It is."

"Ian," Becca said, coming to his and her son's rescue. "This is Jared Donnelly. He's the racer in the picture in Brendon's magazine."

"Aunt Em. You know this guy?" Ian asked, skepticism still coloring his face.

And Connor thought two-year-olds were tough.

"Yes, Ian." Patience laced Jinx's face. "My brother's oldest son," she said as if that explained the little Doubting Thomas. "Jared is a champion racer."

"Former racer. I've retired."

"Get out!" Ian's voice rose with excitement.

"Told you," Brendon said, shooting Jared a triumphant look. "Wait, aren't you and Pastor Connor going to stay and swim with us?"

"Brendon, I think Jared and Pastor Connor have finished swimming, and you and Ian are going to miss out if you don't go and get your buddy tags." Becca pointed to one of the other teachers on the beach handing out colored plastic bracelets.

"See you, Jared. Remember you still owe me a ride on your bike."

"Your mom's going to let you ride on his motorcycle?" Ian said in a loud whisper.

"Why not? Yours lets you ride with your sister Autumn's husband, Dr. Jon."

"Right, but he's a doctor, not a motocross racer."

"Brendon," Becca said.

"Ian," Emily echoed.

"Go," they both ordered.

Connor laughed. "We'll leave you to your charges."

Jared hesitated. He didn't have anything else planned for the rest of the afternoon. "I can stay if you need another person to watch the kids swim."

"No, we're good." Becca quickly dismissed him.

Too quickly for the adolescent longing to feel like he belonged—that he was wanted—here in Paradox Lake. A longing that seemed to surface all too often when she was around. He'd earned that sense of belonging on the motocross circuit where no one knew him as Jerry Donnelly's delinquent kid, and hoped to achieve it here with his racing school.

Chapter Three

"What was that?" Emily asked.

"What was what?" Becca pulled her beach bag up more firmly on her shoulder.

"You and our town celebrity, Jared. Brendon and him being best buddies. Ari talking about him at Sunday school."

Becca scanned the beach for a good spot for them to sit and watch the kids swim.

"The current between you and Jared," Emily prodded.

Becca frowned at her friend. "I ran into him at his grandmother's house when the kids and I stopped there to drop off something for Edna. Brendon recognized Jared from his magazine and asked him to autograph it. Not to be outdone, Ari insisted Jared read her storybook while I went out to the garden with Edna. That's all there is to it. This spot look good to you?" Becca slipped her bag from her shoulder and rummaged in it for the blanket she'd packed. She wasn't going to mention the run-in with Debbie and the Sheriff the next day.

"Ari stayed with him while you went out to the garden. Your Ari? The little girl who insisted you wait on a chair outside her Sunday school room where she could see you for most of last school year? That Ari?"

"She's getting better." Becca had been surprised how her daughter had latched on to Jared. She shook the blanket out hard and let it settle on the ground. Unfortunately, Ari was still asking daily when Jared was going to come and read to her. She pressed her lips together. Ari got enough broken promises from her father.

"What's that sour face about?" Emily dropped to the blanket and sat with her arms wrapped around her knees, scanning the kids swimming in the lake.

"Nothing. I was just thinking."

"About Jared? Not all men are like Matt."

Mentally, Becca knew that was true. Emotionally, it was another story. She and Matt had dated for most of high school and, except for a short breakup, through college. He'd left her when Brendon was a toddler, and she hadn't even realized yet that she was expecting Ari.

Becca sat down next to Emily. "Now, my turn for questions. You and Jared were...are friends?"

"Jealous?"

"No. Maybe. Yes. But not how you think. I would have liked to have known him in high school."

"No, you wouldn't have. You were too busy being pretty and smart and popular. As a teenager, Jared had too much baggage for you to handle. I'm not sure he ever was a teenager."

That had been one of the things that had attracted her to Jared as a teen. He seemed more responsible, mature, even though he was a year younger than her crowd. "I wasn't that superficial."

Emily shook her head. "You were that untried, sheltered. You've lived some now."

"Thank you, Dr. Stacey. I hadn't realized you'd given

up graphic arts for psychology. And you weren't sheltered?"

Emily grinned. "Dad certainly tried. But it didn't carry over to school. Remember, I was the tall, clumsy kid everyone called Jinx. My brother, Neal, is eight years older than I am. He wasn't around school to shelter me after fourth grade."

"And you and Jared?"

"Used to talk sometimes about our misfit lives and how we were going to leave Paradox Lake at our first opportunity. Strictly platonic."

Jared hadn't struck Becca as a misfit then—and certainly didn't now.

Becca's cell phone buzzed that she had a text, giving her a welcome break from the conversation. She checked the screen. *Maybe not.*

"Go ahead and answer," Emily said.

"It's the Sheriff. He recently got a smartphone and has gone text crazy. It's probably nothing." She dropped the phone to the blanket.

"Are he and Debbie still dogging your every move?"

Becca sighed. "Almost more so since he got his new phone. I have an unsettled feeling it has something to do with Matt and my custody agreement. Debbie and the Sheriff are planning to move to Florida now that he's retired. It's making me a wreck. I've prayed, but I can't seem to find the peace I normally would."

"I have just the thing. The Singles Group is challenging the Couples Group in 'Bible Jeopardy' tomorrow night. I don't know how peaceful it will be, but we'll have fellowship, inspiration and food. I'm making my cheesecake brownies. Maybe Connor will bring his big brother."

Jared's presence didn't exactly shout peaceful to Becca. "I can't."

"Mom's watching Isabelle and Ryan. I know she wouldn't mind watching Ari and Brendon, if that's the problem. Ari would stay with her, wouldn't she?"

"Probably, but I have something else going on."

"With Jared? Are you holding out on me?"

"Not with Jared. I have to go to the Town Zoning Board meeting in Schroon Lake."

"Why?"

Becca laughed. "The expression on your face. I'm the newest board member."

"I ask again, why?"

"I was teaching civics and thought I should be more involved. Edna's husband, Harry, mentioned the opening."

Emily shook her head. "Will you ever learn? You don't have to be involved in everything."

"I know. It seemed like a good idea at the time, even after the Sheriff encouraged me to take the seat." Becca's phone rang. She picked it up. "Speaking of the Sheriff, he's probably calling to find out why I didn't text him back."

"I think I'll walk down to the water and test the temperature." Emily stood and slipped off her shoes.

"That's right. Desert me in my time of need." Becca pressed the phone screen to answer the call. "Hello."

"Have you read the agenda for the Zoning Board meeting?"

"No."

"I texted it to you."

"Ken, I'm working."

"Then I'll give you the short version. Your boyfriend wants to build a motocross track on Bert Miller's property."

That was what Jared wanted to use Bert's land for? To build his racetrack? Here in Paradox Lake? She should have made the connection. Her breath caught. A race-track could be almost as bad as a resort casino. In some ways, worse, considering Brendon's current obsession with motorcycles.

"If you know what's good for you, you'll make sure that doesn't happen."

"Are you threatening me?"

"No, but I know how much you hate Family Court." He hung up.

Becca stared at her phone for a moment before touching the text button. She viewed the agenda Ken had photographed and texted her, the sinking feeling in her stomach bottoming out when she reached the fourth bullet point: *Jared Donnelly—request for a recreational development zoning exception to construct a motocross track on parcel 87268 on Conifer Road.*

"What's wrong?" Emily had returned and was standing over her.

"It looks like I will be spending tomorrow evening with Jared after all."

Confusion spread across Emily's face. "You said the call was from Sheriff Norton."

"It was. Apparently, Jared wants to build a motocross track on the land he inherited from Bert Miller. And the Sheriff wants me to stop him."

Jared climbed from the cab of his pickup truck and stood in the newly paved parking lot, taking in the sprawling two-story, redbrick building with its white-columned entrance. The Schroon Town Hall. He slammed the door shut. The smell of the blacktop made his nose twitch. The last time he'd been here had been for court when he was eighteen, to answer his driving-while-impaired charge. The parking lot had been newly tarred that day, too.

His stomach churned. After his arrest, his dad had made a big show about how he was going to be there for Jared. He didn't need a lawyer. Jared still had been naive enough to believe him—or at least to want to believe him. Then, when he and his brothers had gotten home from school the day of his court appearance, he'd found their father passed out in the bedroom, an empty vodka bottle on the bed stand. That was the last time he'd believed his father.

That night, Jared had made burgers and fries for his brothers and him for supper. For whatever reason, he remembered that clearly. But he hadn't been able to choke down more than a bite or two. He'd considered chugging one of the beers his dad had in the refrigerator for courage before remembering that had been what had gotten him in trouble in the first place. Instead, he'd told Josh to help Connor with his homework, and he'd driven illegally to the town hall for court. Keeping his eyes focused forward, he'd walked to the front of the room where court was held, signed in and had taken a seat at the far side, determined to handle whatever happened like a real man. His mother had slipped in beside him just before the public defender had motioned him up to the desk to talk. The scent of the diner lingering on his mother's uniform had somehow reassured him. She'd had no illusions about Jared's father coming through for him.

"Jared."

The sound of his name jerked him back to the present. A light-haired man about his age stepped from a sleek navy blue Mercedes parked near the building.

"Dan, thanks for coming." Jared strode across the parking lot and shook hands with the Albany lawyer he'd hired. Jinx Stacey's sister-in-law, Anne Hazard, had recommended him. Her environmental engineering firm had used Dan on several projects.

"I spoke with the town attorney this afternoon," Dan said. "He saw no problem with your building permit being approved without a public hearing for a variance. It should fall under the recreational development exception to the residential-agriculture zoning classification."

"Great," Jared said with more confidence than he felt. It must have been the lingering bad memories. He glanced at the hall. Neither of them had to be here. Tonight was an ordinary meeting of the Zoning Board. He could wait and call the building inspector in the morning. "In that case, it might better be to let the board go ahead and make their decision without us. The less said the better."

"You don't get off that easy." Dan pressed his key fob to lock his car. "As I told you on the phone, it'll look good to be here to answer any questions the board members may have. The meeting is open, even though it's not an official public hearing."

"Let's get it over with, then."

The two men went inside and entered the nearly empty main meeting room. Not much had changed since the last time he'd been here. He swallowed. He hoped that wasn't indicative of today's outcome. No. This time he wasn't a kid, and he wasn't going to let anyone drive him or his project out of town.

"An empty room." Dan nodded. "Just what I was hoping to see. You've done a good job of keeping your plans for building here under the local radar. These things go better when the public doesn't get involved."

Jared tensed. "My idea is for the track and school to be a community project, not a secret strike on the town." He shifted his weight. Dan had come highly recommended by Anne Hazard. From working with Anne and her staff on the environmental studies for the project, he'd found her very open and up-front. He'd assumed Dan was the same.

"Right. Do you know Steve Monti, the town attorney? We went to law school together."

If the attorney was Dan's age, it couldn't be the same attorney who had orchestrated the Driving While Ability Impaired resolution that had pulled his license for six months and required him to pay restitution to Sheriff Norton. His agreement to leave town quietly right after high school graduation had been unstated—at least in the actual plea bargain.

"No, the name isn't familiar."

"I'll introduce you." Dan raised his hand to catch the attention of a man in a dark suit standing at one end of the dais. He met them halfway across the room.

"Steve Monti. This is Jared Donnelly."

He and the town attorney shook hands.

The attorney stepped away to the other side of Dan. "I may have spoken too soon this afternoon." The town attorney said something else in a low voice that Jared didn't catch.

"The paperwork is all in order."

Despite Dan's assertion, Jared's throat tightened.

"It is, but one of the board members lives near the development site. She's insisting on a public hearing before the building permit is approved."

"Becca."

The other two men looked at Jared. He hadn't realized he'd spoken his thought. But it couldn't be. With her job and the kids, she had more than enough to keep her busy. It must be one of the other Conifer Road residents.

"Yes, Becca Norton. She's new to the board. You know her?" Steve asked.

He cleared his throat. "Yes, but not like we're close friends or anything." That sounded lame.

"It might be more to your benefit if she were. She has connections. Her father-in-law was the county Sheriff."

"Ex-father-in-law."

Dan silently scrutinized him.

"I know the Sheriff, too." *And he has to be behind this somehow.*

"Steve, we're ready to start." Jared recognized the man speaking as the owner of the diner where his mother used to work. For a moment, he was eighteen again, alone against the world.

"Time to make our case." Dan slapped him on the back, reminding him he wasn't alone. This time, he had a team behind him. A team *he'd* put together. And the resources to back that team.

Jared turned to Dan. "Did you get a copy of the meeting agenda?"

Since they appeared to be the only permit applicants here, he hoped the board would get to them first. He'd just as soon get this over with and get out of here.

"Yeah." He grinned. "You are the agenda."

"Come on down," Tom Hill, the chair of the Zoning Board boomed, reminiscent of *The Price Is Right*. "Take a seat. We're not formal here."

Becca kept her gaze lowered as the men approached the dais. She placed the paper she held in her hands on the flat surface in front of her and smoothed it. Anger at herself for caving in to the Sheriff's demand warred with concern for her kids and the life she was trying to build for them. She flicked the corner of the sheet with her index finger. The uneasiness she felt about Jared's project wasn't limited to her. She'd run into one of her two neighbors at the gas station convenience store. When Becca had mentioned that she was on her way to the Zoning Board meeting, he'd asked her what she knew about Jared wanting to build a motocross track on their road and then shared his apprehensions about the potential noise, traffic and strangers. He'd also reminded her how the Conifer Road residents had banded together to oppose the casino if it had been proposed.

"And this is our newest board member, Rebecca Norton," Tom said.

She looked up into Jared's deep blue eyes. They darkened, almost as if he'd read her thoughts about the track. But that was ridiculous.

"Hi, Jared."

"Becca. What a pleasant surprise."

He wouldn't think so for long. Her pulse quickened. Or maybe he was being sarcastic and didn't think that now, either. Although his tone wasn't sarcastic, she didn't know him well enough to read the real meaning of his words any more than he'd been reading her thoughts a moment ago.

Tom cleared his throat. "Now that introductions are over, I think we can get this done in quick order."

Jared relaxed his stance. "We brought updated plans and the preliminary environmental studies from Green-Spaces for you to look over." He stepped to the dais to hand a cardboard tube holding the plans to the board members.

Tom took the tube and waved him off. "That won't be necessary tonight. I don't know what Steve told your guy." He nodded at Dan. "But Ms. Norton has raised new questions from her and one of the other property owners on Conifer Road. We've decided a public hearing is necessary. Your development may not fall under the recreational facility exception, after all—it being a racing school rather than a resort or simply a racetrack open to the public."

The town attorney shuffled his feet while Jared's attorney glared at her. But their actions barely registered. She was focused on Jared. He seemed to be looking past her to something on the wall behind the dais. She resisted the urge to turn and see what he was looking at, only to regret that decision. If she had, she would have missed the gut-wrenching hardening of his features. She started to slump in her seat, then straightened and crossed her arms. Even if she felt bad for Jared, who obviously wanted to get started on his project, she had valid reasons for pushing the public hearing. And for him, it could deflect opposition later, after he'd already sunk money into the motocross track.

"The hearing will be two weeks from Tuesday, our usual meeting night," the board chair said. "Same time as tonight. That'll let us get the required notices in the *Times of Ti.* You'll get a letter in the mail."

"Thank you," Jared's attorney said. "We'll see you in two weeks."

Jared jerked a nod in the direction of the board before he strode from the room.

Becca watched him until he reached the doorway. She pulled her shoulder bag from the back of her chair and rose as he disappeared into the hall. "If we're done, I need to get home. The kids, you know."

Becca hated to use the kids as an excuse. She rarely did. But she needed to speak with Jared, to explain her concerns about the motocross track. She could only hope that he and his lawyer might be talking outside.

"Sure," Tom said. "That's all the business we had for tonight. Glad to have you on board." He chuckled at his pun and looked to the other members for affirmation. "We need more younger people to be involved in town government."

She smiled while inwardly chaffing at the extra minute his short speech added to the head start Jared had on her. "Thanks. It's my community. I want to do what I can." *And not alienate Jared Donnelly doing it.*

Becca crossed the room as quickly as she could without looking as though she was running from the hall. Stepping into the warm cloudy night, she scanned the parking lot for Jared. There were four cars besides hers and four board members still in the hall. Her heart sank. He was gone. A cloud passed in front of the full moon casting shadows on the car. Gray shadows. Like her mood.

She unlocked her car and started it. Her concerns about having a motocross track almost in her backyard were real, although the magazine article and Tom Hill had called it a motocross school, not a track. She shouldn't feel so agitated about having brought those concerns up to the board. She and other people in the community who would be affected by Jared's proposed project deserved to learn more. Except Jared's stony expression when Tom had told him about the public hearing kept flashing in her mind. The expression had made Jared look incredibly attractive and threatening at the same time.

Becca slowed the car in front of the Paradox Lake General Store. Brendon had finished the last of the milk at dinner. As she pulled in to stop to get some more, a motorcycle parked in the lot grabbed her attention. She replayed her son's chatter about Jared's bike in her head. She tilted her chin down and frowned at the vehicle.

Brendon had said Jared's bike was lime green. This one was dark blue, and the middle-aged man who was walking toward it definitely wasn't Jared. She went into the store and headed directly to the coolers at the far right where the dairy products were.

Pulling the glass door open with her left hand, she reached in for one of the gallon containers of milk in the back of the cooler, releasing the door to close gently against her so she could bend in far enough to grab it. She sensed someone behind her and stiffened even before she felt the person grasp the door to hold it open for her. Not to be unfriendly, but she hoped it was a helpful tourist rather than anyone she knew. She wasn't in a mood for idle chat.

"Thanks," she said without looking as she turned to walk to the checkout.

"No problem," said the one person she did want to talk to.

Looking back at Jared and his controlled features, she swallowed. Or the one person she'd *thought* she wanted to talk to.

Jared's heart twisted in unison with Becca's scowl. He should have known things were going too smoothly. Although he'd done all his prep work carefully, he'd expected some opposition to his plans. But Becca Norton wasn't the person he'd pictured spearheading it.

"Thanks," she said again, her expression looking more pensive now that she'd turned fully toward him. "I didn't realize it was you."

"Like I didn't realize you were on the Zoning Board."

Becca's hint of a smile disappeared. He could have kicked himself for not guarding his words. He needed to woo, not alienate Becca. Woo her in the sense of convincing her of the good his motocross school would do. Any other wooing was out of the question. He studied her heart-shaped face for a moment. As if he, a Donnelly, would have any chance with a woman like Becca. He shook off his pity trip back in time. "That didn't come out quite right."

"It's okay. Do you have a couple of minutes to talk? I'll check this out." She raised the gallon of milk she held. "And we can get a cup of coffee or something."

"Sure. I need to pick up some coffee for the morning, too." Jared walked to the grocery shelf and grabbed a large can of coffee, then put it back in favor of a smaller bag of a special dark roast. He made his way to the checkout at the front of the store and looked around.

Becca motioned to him from one of the tables in the deli area. "Over here. You did want coffee, right? I have it covered." A waitress who looked vaguely familiar placed two heavy mugs on the table in front of her.

He ground his teeth. Not that he was a chauvinist. But he was used to being the one who picked up the tab, did for others. What she was earning at the day-care center, or as a high school teacher, for that matter, couldn't come close to the income from his invested race winnings. His fingers tightened around the bag of coffee. *That* sounded too much like his money-obsessed brother Josh.

"You remember Lori Lyons." Becca smiled at the waitress.

"Sure, I do." Lori had been another one of the untouchables on the cheerleading squad with Becca. "I was sorry to hear about Stan."

"Thank you," Lori said. "I appreciated your card."

Becca knitted her brows in question.

When Jared had heard about Lori's husband Stan's death in a NASCAR accident shortly after he'd lost a close friend on the motocross circuit, he'd felt a connection to Lori and had shot her off a sympathy card. "My grandmother told me about Stan's accident," he said in explanation.

Becca's expression turned thoughtful. He'd have to be careful or he'd lose his tough-guy image.

"I'd love to catch up," Lori said. "But my shift is done and I need to pick the girls up from Stan's mother's house. She babysits for me when I have to work during the evening." She turned to Jared. "I have ten-year-old twins. I usually work days, so I have to get them up early for day care tomorrow."

Jared scuffed his toe against the table leg. Lori was being a little too friendly for him. They hadn't been friends in school and, as callous as it sounded, he'd sent her the sympathy card as much as a way to work through his own grief as a true condolence.

"I'll see you in the morning, Becca," Lori said. "And why don't *you*—" she pointed at Jared "—stop by after the lunch rush some afternoon this week. I'd love to hear about your time on the circuit." She shot a dazzling smile his way and gave him a flirty wave before walking back behind the counter and into the kitchen.

Yep, way too friendly, which he couldn't say about Becca, given her dark frown. Unless she was jealous of Lori. They had been rivals in school. He yanked out the chair across the table from Becca. Only in his mind. The source of Becca's frown more likely could be chalked up to his plans for the racing school and Lori getting in the way of Becca speaking her mind about it.

He slid into the chair and wrapped his hands around the coffee mug. "I take it you want to talk about the track."

"I do." The sip of coffee she took sweetened her frown

into what could almost be called a smile. "I hope you don't mind that I ordered your coffee. It's a regular." She glanced at the specialty coffee he'd bought. "But maybe you'd like something different."

He lifted the bag of coffee. "This is for Connor. I'm good with anything black that doesn't taste like motor oil."

She took another sip of her coffee and gazed at him over the rim of the cup, her brown eyes colored with apprehension. "The Zoning Board's decision surprised you."

He bit his tongue before he said something he'd regret. "Right. The town attorney had told my attorney everything looked like a go. That there wouldn't be a need for a public hearing."

"That's my fault."

He took a healthy draw of his coffee and waited.

"I didn't get the agenda for the meeting until yesterday afternoon, and what I got didn't have a lot of details. With work and the kids, I didn't have time to do any research. Evidently, the other board members and the town attorney already had discussed it. Tonight was my first board meeting."

"Yeah. Dan, my attorney, and I had felt out the town building inspector about the project a while ago, before I'd decided on a spot to build it."

"That spot being my backyard."

"Not exactly your backyard." He'd made a tactical error not sounding out the property owners on Conifer Road about his idea when Bert had first written him about his intention to leave him the acreage. But it had seemed like everything was coming together for him. He looked across the table. *Until now.*

"Close enough for me and some of my neighbors to have some questions."

"Ask away." He leaned back in his seat.

"Why? Why come back here when you could go anywhere?"

He worked to maintain his casual pose, while a small blaze lit inside him. From her words, it sounded to him as if she was as opposed to him being in Paradox Lake as she was to him building his racing school here. He'd thought better of her. Correction. He'd thought better of the image of Becca he held in his head from high school. An image that could be all wrong.

"Yes, I could go anywhere. I could build the school and motocross track here and run it from somewhere else. Let me ask you a question. Is it the racing school or me you have a problem with?"

Becca blanched and he slunk down in his chair. What had gotten into him, jumping to a dumb conclusion like that? He knew. He wanted this project to succeed with the same competitive hunger that had made him a champion racer. And the stakes here were greater than any race's.

"I'm sorry if that's how I sounded."

The contrition in her voice tore at him worse than her misinterpreted question.

"I'll start over. My neighbors and I have some valid concerns about a motocross track near our homes, some of the same concerns we had when Bert Miller was considering selling his property to a syndicate bidding on a state gambling license."

Becca was equating his racing school for needy kids to a gambling casino? The banked flame in his belly reignited.

"Other people in the community may have issues, too.

I thought it would help me if I knew why you wanted to build it here."

"Understandable. I…"

The ring of her cell phone interrupted him.

She pulled the phone from her pocket and glanced at it. "I have to take it. It could be about the kids."

Jared finished his coffee while Becca listened to the person at the other end of the call.

"That was Debbie. My daughter's running a temperature. I have to go."

"I hope Ari's okay."

Becca stood and scooped up her purse. "It's probably just a summer cold."

He pushed his chair back. "Let me know if you want to get together to talk about your concerns before the public forum. I can show you the plans and tell you more about them."

"Okay. I'll call you at Connor's. You do understand that it's not personal."

"Of course." He walked her out and they parted at her car. The problem was that it was personal for him—both his reasons for wanting to build the school and track in Paradox Lake *and* the urge he'd had earlier to pull Becca into his arms and comfort her when she'd blanched at his sharp question.

Chapter Four

Jared flung the *Times of Ti* on the couch. So that's why Becca hadn't called. She'd had no intention of hearing more about the motocross school from him before launching her campaign against it. The news article didn't mention names, but it said a group of Conifer Road residents had organized against the project. That had to include her. Only three families lived on Conifer Road. Jared didn't know the other two. He'd hoped that after he and Becca had talked, she'd be his in with the other families to calm any objections they might have.

"Hey, big bro, what's with the face?" Connor crossed the living room, picked up the weekly newspaper and skimmed the lead article. "I see."

"No, I don't think you do."

"Come on. You grew up here. You had to expect some opposition. Some people don't want any changes, even those for the better."

Jared grabbed the paper from him. "But no one has given me a chance to tell them it's for the better, to explain how it'll benefit the community. I figured I'd get that at the public hearing next week. The project could be dead by then." He jabbed a finger at the front page.

"Look at the headline, 'Conifer Road Residents Rise Up Against Motocross Track.'"

Connor shrugged. "Okay, the headline is a little sensationalized. From what I saw, all the article says is that the residents have questions to raise at the public hearing."

Jared ignored his brother's placating. "And the photo of the *No Racetrack* bumper sticker with the X through a silhouette of a bike racer is a nice touch. She must have rushed right out the day after the Zoning Board meeting and had them printed."

"By she, I take it you mean Becca. Can you blame her or her neighbors? You're planning to build something big in their neighborhood."

"Whose side are you on, anyway?"

"Yours. You need to back off if you want to win support for your racetrack."

"It's a school, not a racetrack." Jared glared at Connor.

"Hey, I have a good idea what this project means to you, but, like I said, lighten up. And, if you want to see your dream succeed, you should socialize with the locals instead of spending your time holed up here."

Jared breathed in and out to release some of his tension. "I know. But I'll admit it's hard. I have a lot of bad memories, and I suspect a fair number of the locals do, too."

Connor broke into a smile. "You'd be surprised how much your professional success has done to fade those memories."

"But not mine." Jared tapped his fingers against his thigh.

"You're too hard on yourself. And not to criticize, but calling Becca back would have been a good start on cultivating local support."

"Say what?"

"If you'd called Becca back, you might have had a chance to tell her more about your plans before she talked to the paper. *If* she talked to the paper. I didn't see her name anywhere."

Jared took a step toward Connor. "Are you saying Becca called?"

"Sure, the morning after the Zoning Board meeting. You'd gone into Ticonderoga to meet with the environmental engineer at GreenSpaces. It was just before I got the call that Sid Blasnik was having emergency surgery and drove up to Saranac Lake to sit with his wife at the medical center. I left you a note on the counter."

"I didn't see any note."

"I'm sure I told you when I got back."

"You didn't." Jared reined in the urge to shake his little brother. Connor didn't know how important her calling was to him. More important than it had any reason to be.

"Sorry. Call her and tell her I didn't give you the message."

"I could do that." But he wasn't sure he would. It might be better to wait it out and hear all of the opposition's concerns and address them, rather than make it something personal between him and Becca.

"Do you have plans for tonight?" Connor asked.

"Huh?" His brother's abrupt change of topic disoriented him.

"The Singles Group and the Couples Group at church are playing their second round of Bible trivia. The Couples Group creamed us last time. We could use some new blood."

Jared still wasn't sure how they'd gotten from Becca's phone call to "Bible Jeopardy," and it must have shown in his expression.

"To socialize, cultivate support," Connor said in a patient tone Jared was certain he must have learned in the seminary. The kid Jared had left behind when he'd exited Paradox Lake had been anything but patient.

He gave in. "Why not?"

Connor hadn't said anything, but Jared knew his brother was hurt that he hadn't attended Hazardtown Community Church since he'd returned to Paradox Lake. He hadn't been able to shake the old feelings that the people at church—people his parents' age and older who'd known his father—would be silently judging him, and he'd come up lacking, just like his father. Those feelings were one of the reasons he'd made his past visits home short and infrequent. But he wasn't here for a visit. He was here for good. It was more than time to banish the shadows of the past.

"Great." Connor slapped him on the back. "Josh should be there along with Emily Stacey and some others you may know from school. Of course, most of them are our competition in the Couples Group."

Jared caught a wistful note in the emphasis his brother put on "the Couples Group." More power to Connor if he thought marriage could be in his future. And who was he to think it couldn't be just because he couldn't see it in his? Connor was seven years younger than he was, maybe young enough that he wasn't as scarred by memories of their father as Jared was. Or maybe he had a greater trust in God than Jared had managed to forge despite all his efforts, and could forgive and move on.

"I'm glad you talked me into this," Becca said, as she got out of Emily's car in the Hazardtown Community Church parking lot.

"I didn't have to do much talking."

"You're right. Teaching day care is a lot different than

teaching high school history. I need some adult time so badly that it was worth putting up with the Sheriff's accolades about my interview in the *Times of Ti* when I dropped off the kids there after work. An interview that, incidentally, I didn't give. Nor did I have anything to do with the bumper stickers. You've seen them?"

"Yeah. What's with Ken and Jared?" Emily asked. "I can see your opposition to the racetrack, it being so close to your house. You'd have to put up with all the added traffic and all of the other stuff that comes with a tourist attraction nearby. I can't see why Ken is all up in arms about it. Aren't he and Debbie planning to move to Florida anyway?"

Becca swung the car door shut with more force than necessary. "I'm not against Jared's racetrack. I do have concerns because it would be so close to my house, and I want to get more information about it before I decide whether I'm for or against it." At least, that's what she kept telling herself, that she was keeping an open mind until she knew more details. More details she already could have if Jared had returned her phone call.

"As for the Sheriff, who knows why he thinks the way he does about anything?" she said. "He seems to have a personal dislike of Jared, though."

Becca paused while she waited for Emily to walk around the front of the car and join her on the sidewalk that led to the church hall. For a split second, she toyed with the thought of telling Emily about the implied accusation the Sheriff had made about her and Jared. She needed some way to release the outrage pent up inside her. Emily was a close and trusted friend. But Becca had never been one to share her inner self, not even, she had to admit, with her ex-husband. When she was younger, it was prompted by a fear that people might not like the real Becca beneath the perfect facade. Now, maybe it was more of a habit not to share.

"Jared did do a pretty good job of demolishing the Nortons' mailbox and front fence with his car after a night of partying in high school," Emily said. "My brother emailed me about it when I was away at college because he knew Jared and I were sort of friends."

Remarks the Sheriff had made about Jared's offtrack life when he'd bought Brendon his magazine ran through Becca's mind. *Parties, women, drinking.* She went cold. Just like Matt. While her ex-in-laws had turned a blind eye to their son's behavior, she'd lived with it the last year and a half of her marriage.

"Lose that look. It was years ago, and I know other kids around here who have done a lot worse."

"I'm sure." Becca pulled the handle of the door to the hall and swung it open for Emily. *Things I wouldn't want my kids doing.* She realized that since she and Jared had met in the meadow, she'd been lionizing him in her mind, just like Brendon. What did she really know about Jared or what he planned to do? At the General Store after the Zoning Board meeting, he'd made it sound as though he was as eager to tell her about his project as she was to hear about. And she'd believed him until he hadn't bothered to return her call.

"We usually meet in the lounge," Emily said. "I wonder what kind of turnout we'll have tonight. Since Drew's too busy with the camp during the summer to make the meetings, I had to play on the Singles Group team last match to help even things out. But they were still outnumbered, and the Couples Group creamed us."

"If I remember correctly, you hate losing."

"I like to think of it more as I love winning. Connor

said he was going to drum up more singles for tonight. His brothers, at least."

Becca hadn't considered Jared might be here. Her stomach sank. She'd come for some relaxing socialization. She picked up her pace. And she wasn't going to let Jared Donnelly unsettle her and spoil that.

"With Connor playing for the singles and you and your steel-trap mind of Biblical knowledge, we might see some real competition tonight."

"What can I say?" Becca tried for a light carefree tone she didn't feel. "The Bible is a living history and history is my passion." Somehow, her words saddened her.

"Emily, Becca." Connor met them in the hall in front of the lounge. "Go on in. I thought I'd put some coffee on in the hall kitchen for those of us who may need a boost after the competition. You're the first to arrive, except for Jared and me."

Becca hung back behind Emily. So Jared had come.

"I'll help you," Emily said.

Confusion spread across Connor's face until Emily nodded at Becca and toward the lounge.

A smile replaced the confusion. "Right. Help me. In the kitchen."

Becca grit her teeth. Emily probably thought she was doing her a favor leaving her alone with Jared. She pasted a smile on her face and walked into the lounge. But it was a favor she could do without.

"Becca." Jared rose as she entered the room. "Hi. Connor didn't say you'd be here tonight."

"He didn't know. I decided at the last minute. I haven't been to the Singles Group in a while."

Jared wiped his hands on his jeans and watched her take a seat on the couch next to the chair where he'd been sitting. She folded her hands in her lap and looked up at him, her face expressionless. He sat back down.

"Uh, Connor said you called the other day."

She met his gaze with the same bland visage. "You got my message, then."

"Yes, but not until today. Connor said he'd left me a note, but I didn't see it."

Her eyes brightened. Or at least he thought they had.

"I would have called back if I'd known sooner."

"That's okay."

He caught a hint of skepticism in her words and, remembering his anger when he'd thought she'd blown him off, couldn't blame her for feeling the same about his not calling back. But the news article was something else, something that justified anger. She'd spoken publicly without having all of the facts. "I saw the article in the *Times*."

Her mouth twisted as if she'd tasted something sour. "I didn't talk to anyone at the newspaper."

The speed of her denial raised a red flag in his mind. He calculated what her words might be hiding. His best guess was that she and her neighbors had gotten together and someone else, acting as spokesperson, had talked to the reporter. He crossed his arms in front of his chest. If he'd gotten the message about Becca's call, he might have been able to neutralize the news report and be on a more even footing for the public hearing.

"But it expresses your opinion."

She unclasped and clasped her hands. "I didn't say that."

No, she hadn't. He didn't know what was making him feel so adversarial, except he wanted to know what she thought so he could counter her opposition.

"Hey." His brother Josh poked his head in the lounge. "Is this a private conversation or can anyone join in?"

"Anyone's welcome," Becca said.

Jared worked a muscle in his jaw. For all he'd missed his family—most of them, at least—when he'd been on the circuit, he'd forgotten how having family around meant them being *around*. And Becca's being so quick to welcome his brother made Jared think she'd changed her mind about hearing him out about his plans, if she'd even wanted to in the first place.

"Connor and Emily are in the hall kitchen making coffee," she said.

"Nope. Emily's right here." She entered the lounge with her brother, Neal; his wife, Anne; and another couple.

"Jared, I don't think you know Jamie and Eli Peyton," she said. "They're members of the Couples Group."

"Ah, the great Jared Donnelly," Jamie said with a wide grin, as she and the others sat down. "My son is one of your biggest fans."

Her husband nodded. "Myles has been scheming to meet you since he found out you were in town. Him and every boy in the church Youth Group and my summer school math class."

Jared shifted in his seat, anxious to steer the conversation away from himself. "So you teach with Becca."

"I work with Becca. I'm the high school guidance counselor. But the school had trouble getting a teacher for summer school math. I'm certified, so I agreed."

"I could use your professional expertise with kids," Jared said. "For a project I'm working on." It might be easier to share his intentions for building the motocross school and track with Becca by telling Eli and the others about it.

"For your motocross track. I can't see how I could help."

Jared took a moment to determine whether he'd caught an edge to the other man's voice or had imagined it.

"We were talking about that on the way over," Jamie said before Jared could answer her husband. "And how it would impact the traffic on State Route 74. We live just off the highway."

Anne leaned forward in her chair. "The traffic study GreenSpaces did as part of our environmental study showed minimal impact in your area. Most of the traffic would be coming north on US Route 9 or off the Northway Interstate and up 9."

Jared leaned back in his seat. He'd lost his perfect segue into talking about helping kids and the community to a discussion of traffic patterns. He glanced at Becca, who sat tight lipped, listening. Traffic patterns that would bring more vehicles past her house.

"We're doing some further study," his brother Josh added. "To see if a traffic circle will be needed at the corner of Conifer Road to handle the track traffic."

Becca's eyes widened.

The traffic circle was news to Jared. He cracked his knuckles. Josh could have said something to him about it before now.

Anne's eyes narrowed. "That recommendation is very preliminary. There may be no need for a circle."

Josh stiffened at his employer's admonishment, and Jared sympathized with him, even though a moment earlier he been ready to gag him before he said something else that might upset Becca. Josh never did anything halfway, or lost an opportunity to make himself look good. He was into his work and wanted to tell everyone what he knew.

"But you do expect the track to cause significantly more traffic up my way," Becca said.

"It's a racing school, for kids, not a track," Jared corrected, his irritation getting the best of him. Everyone, his brother included, seemed to be missing that detail.

The room quieted.

He had his opening. "Here's what I'm planning—"

Connor strode into the lounge, interrupting Jared mid-sentence. "Sorry to keep you waiting. We got sidetracked talking about some Administrative Council business." He introduced the new arrivals who'd walked in with him. "Everyone ready to get started?"

"In a minute," Eli said. "Jared was telling us about his plans for the racing school."

"Yeah," Connor said. "This might be something cool for you and Drew to get the Youth Group involved in."

Connor gave Jared a nod-up that made him feel like a preschooler getting a "good job" from Mommy.

"Go ahead," Connor said.

As if he needed his baby brother's permission to talk. Jared swallowed his annoyance and explained his plans for a racing school loosely based on the Boys & Girls Clubs. "It's not just about racing. It's about character development and having a safe place to learn." As he made each of his points, he glanced at Becca, buoyed by the interest he read in her eyes.

"And good role models, particularly for teenage boys who don't have a father or other close male relative around," he finished.

Jamie nodded. "I know how important that is." She smiled at her husband. "I don't know where my son would be if Eli hadn't come back to Paradox Lake and taken the counseling position at Schroon Lake Central. Myles's father was killed in Afghanistan when Myles was in middle school."

Jared tried to decipher the shadow that passed over Becca's face at Jamie's words. It wasn't as if Brendon didn't have a father. And his grandfather was in his life. Jared's personal dislike of Ken Norton aside, the man was well respected in the community and it seemed like he could be a male influence in Brendon's life.

"I'm sorry for your loss," Jared said.

The tender look that passed between Eli and Jamie hit Jared square in the heart. He cleared his throat. "The most important lesson of many valuable lessons I learned from my racing mentor was that I had to take charge and have direction in my life both spiritually—" Jared smiled to himself when Connor raised an eyebrow to that "—and professionally."

A hum of agreement buzzed around the room. That hadn't been too bad. Maybe the public hearing wouldn't be, either.

"Not every kid is going to be a motocross champion," one of the men who'd come in with Connor said.

Jared fortified himself with a deep breath. "Not every kid who plays football is going to go pro or every Boy Scout will make Eagle Scout or every girl in the high school ski club will go on to win a gold medal. It's what they learn doing those things that prepares them for life."

Jared did a fast check around the room to see if he sounded as sappy to everyone else as he had to himself. *Good*. No one was smirking. It *was* how he felt.

"That's reasonable," the guy said. "How would your program work?"

As Jared ticked off the basic points of his program, he caught Connor and some of the others glancing at the clock. They probably wanted to get their meeting and game started. He wrapped up and waited for Connor to take over, feeling jazzed at the group's positive reaction to his vision for the racing school.

"Clear something up for me." Becca's voice jarred him out of his bubble of self-satisfaction. "The racetrack is for the kids to practice on. That's it?"

From her hopeful tone, Jared knew what she wanted him to say, and he wanted to be able to say it. To have her behind the project with him. But he couldn't. "No. I hope to schedule some commercial races, maybe attract an American Motocross Association event or two."

The hopeful light left her eyes.

He scrambled to recover his earlier excitement about people getting what it was he wanted to do. "That's the second prong of the project, economic development. The area needs more jobs. The track could provide some." There it was clear and simple and, from the expressions on most of the people's faces, they agreed. Except for Becca. He had a sinking feeling he'd lost her again. If he'd ever had her. She was the only one here who'd be directly affected by the school's location. His mind churned. It wasn't too late to look at other property in the area.

Connor stepped to the center of the room. "We should get things rolling here. I'm sure Jared would be happy to answer any other questions about his racing school after our meeting."

It had to be his imagination, but to Jared it looked like his brother was speaking directly to Becca. Was that Connor's idea of playing matchmaker? He shook it off. His brother wasn't matchmaking. The only one interested in matching him up with Becca was the remnants of his adolescent ego. Connor was cultivating the crowd as he'd told Jared to do. Second thoughts plagued him. Maybe the school wasn't the great idea he thought it was. Too many people to please. He could start a foundation instead and donate money. Clean, direct. Like hopping on his bike at the starting line and heading for the finish. No explanations needed. No crowds to please.

"It looks like we have enough couples and singles to pair up and compete in teams of twos. I assume the married couples want to compete together." Connor made a comical face daring them to disagree. "To free me to play tonight, Tessa Hamilton has volunteered to be emcee for our competition." He nodded at one of the women who had come in with him.

"All you single guys write your names on these slips of paper and put them in this coffee mug. Then, the women will draw partners." He pulled the papers from his jeans pocket and passed them out along with a Sharpie marker.

Jared scratched his name on his slip and dropped it in the mug when it was passed to him.

Connor put his slip in last and handed the mug to Emily. "Hope you don't mind playing for the singles again."

"Not at all if I draw you for my partner." She pulled a paper from the mug and started to open it.

"No." Connor stopped her. "Wait. Don't open it until everyone has drawn a name."

The mug went around the room with Becca drawing last.

"Okay, open them."

"Yes," Emily said. "I pulled Connor. This will make it worth being a single again for the night."

"I'll be sure to tell your husband that," her brother said dryly.

She made a face at him. "We're going to be the pair to beat."

"All I can say is I'm glad you're on our side," Josh said

as he switched seats to sit next to the little blonde who'd picked his name.

Jared vaguely recognized her as the younger sister of one of the guys in his high school class. He searched the faces of the three remaining woman. When his gaze reached Becca, a slow smile spread across her face. She waved the paper with his name at him and his pulse quickened. A couple of minutes ago she had been shooting holes in his plans. And now she was... What *was* she up to?

Chapter Five

The stunned expression on Jared's face said she hadn't lost it, at least not completely. She still could put a guy off his game if she made the effort. And she was going to. Tonight was her much-needed adult time, her fun for the week. Jared and his racetrack weren't going to take that from her. "Ready, partner?"

Without missing a beat, he matched her smile. "As ready as you are."

The warmth of his smile radiated through her.

"Let's open with prayer," Connor said. Everyone stood and clasped hands.

Becca bowed her head and tried to ignore Jared's warm and work-roughened hand encircling hers so she could concentrate on Pastor Connor's words.

"Dear Lord, thank You for bringing us together tonight for fun and fellowship. May our friendly competition help us learn more about You and Your plan for us. In Your name, Amen."

"Amen," Becca echoed. Jared squeezed her hand before he released it, sending a current up her arm. Or had she imagined the squeeze? She flexed her hand, and Jared grinned. She hadn't. Her thoughts scattered. He had her off balance again. She really needed to get out among grown-ups more before she completely forgot how to function as a rational adult in social situations. Her life had become totally centered on the kids and work with nothing just for her. She scooted back into her chair.

"Okay, everyone," Tessa said. "Here are the rules Pastor Connor worked out. I read the question. You and your partner figure out the answer and write it on one of the index cards I'm passing out—along with the Bible book, chapter and verse—the answer is from."

Groans came from a couple corners of the room.

"What did you expect?" Connor said. "It is Bible trivia. And with this group I told Tessa not to make the questions too easy."

"Thanks, bro," Josh said.

Tessa began moving around the room handing out cards. "When you have the answer written, raise your hand, and I'll call on you and come over and read your answer." She surveyed the room. "Looks like I know everyone here. If you answer incorrectly, all the teams in the other group get to collaborate on the answer. For anyone who needs a pen, I have those, too, courtesy of the Strand," Tessa said. "Advertising."

"The movie theater. That brings back some memories," Jared said.

"I inherited it from my grandfather," Tessa said as she handed him a pen and a couple of cards. "You probably don't remember me. I spent a few summers with my grandparents here. Grandma is a friend of your grandmother's. We used to come over to her house."

Jared's expression turned thoughtful, triggering a misplaced envy in Becca that Tessa had a past with him.

"One summer, when I was fifteen or sixteen, you were often there working on a bike."

His eyes lit. "Yes, you were always asking me questions."

"That would be me," Tessa said.

The envy gnawed at her. She'd known Tessa for a couple of years, and Tessa had never said anything about knowing Jared. Becca bit her lip. She was being ridiculous. Why would Tessa have? It wasn't as if Jared had ever come up in their conversations.

"Did you ever get that bike running?" Tessa asked.

"I did. In fact, it still runs."

"You still have it? Cool."

"A man never forgets his first love."

Tessa laughed and moved on.

Becca drummed her fingers on the soft armrest of the couch. Of course, Jared's first love would be a motorcycle. Something she couldn't have shared with him then or be a part of now. Bikes were what Jared did. Who he was. And she was afraid of them.

"How do you want to do this?" Becca asked, pointing to the cards Jared held.

"First, we can work together better if you move over here." Jared slid to the left on the couch, leaving her space next to the end table.

Becca moved the short distance from the chair to the couch and sat as close to the armrest and table as possible without looking as though she was purposely trying to sit as far apart from Jared as she could. One side of his mouth tipped up and her stomach flip-flopped. She picked up the slip of paper with his name, perturbed at his ability to make her think and act like one of her freshman history students.

"Want me to do the writing?" she asked.

"Yeah, you probably noticed mine verges on barely legible."

She studied the writing on the slip for a moment. "On the positive side, your penmanship is bold."

"I hold my pen or pencil wrong," he said. "That's what my elementary school teachers kept telling me."

Becca had the distinct feeling that he'd continued to because they'd told him it was wrong.

"And I had more than one teacher both in school and Sunday school who told me I was too bold for my own good."

She relaxed against the back of the couch as much as she could with him sitting inches away. "Do you have a problem listening to teachers?"

"Not all teachers," he drawled, his gaze trained on her face.

She swallowed twice to relieve her parched throat. "That's good because I've scoped out the competition. Jamie and Eli are our biggest competition in the Couples Group. I know they try to do a daily Bible study with their kids after dinner. We need to work together if we're going to best them. No showboating."

"Even if I didn't know you were a teacher, I'd know you're a teacher."

Becca took that as a compliment. The thing about herself she had the most confidence in was her ability as a teacher. "Are you with me?"

"Definitely."

His enthusiasm made her inch farther into the corner of the couch. What was she doing? It was only a game. He was talking about the game, not about her personally.

"How strong are you at knowing the Bible verses that go with the Bible stories?" she asked.

"I can pinpoint the book."

"Good, then I should be able to find the verse. I speed-read."

"A woman of many talents."

Becca checked his expression for sarcasm, but what she saw looked more like admiration. She turned and lifted her Bible from the end table. "Connor and Emily are our strongest support in the Singles Group. If we're not certain of our answer, we may want to wait a second to see if they raise their hands."

"I can hold my own against my brother."

"But we're playing with him, not against him."

Jared raised his hands in mock surrender.

"Any questions before Tessa reads the first question?" Connor asked. "No?" He looked around the room. "Then, game on."

"First question," Tessa said. "How many demons came out of Mary Magdalene?"

"Seven," Becca wrote on a card without even having to think.

"Luke," Jared whispered in her ear. "Eight, I think."

Becca turned right to *Luke* and skimmed the page. She shot her left hand into the air while she wrote *Eight: two* with her right.

"Becca." Tessa recognized her, walked over and read the card. "Correct. Do you or Jared want to read the verse?"

Jared gave Becca a nod.

"'And also some women who had been cured of evil spirits and diseases: Mary (called Magdalene) from whom seven demons had come out.'"

"All right. Not to show my allegiance, but the Singles are on the board."

Jared smiled. "See, I can be a team player."

"True." And she was enjoying him being on her team a little too much.

"Now, on to question two," Tessa said.

That one went to Jamie and Eli for the Couples Group. They played on neck and neck with the Couples Group, taking the second-to-last question to make the game a tie.

"The deciding question is…" Tessa paused for drama. "At the battle of Gath there was a giant with 24 fingers and toes. Who killed him?"

"That's a tough one," Becca said. "I have no idea."

"I do." Jared grabbed the last card from her and she handed him the pen. He scrawled *Jonathan* on the card, along with *1 Chronicles*.

Becca already had her Bible open. "Any idea what book?"

He grimaced. "Toward the end."

"Got it." She pointed to the page and he quickly wrote *Twenty: six and seven* before raising his hand.

"Jared, Josh." Tessa swung her head from one brother to the other. "I don't know which of you had your hand up first. Good thing you're on the same team."

Jared tensed when Josh looked at him. The room went quiet.

From her many boy cousins, Becca knew how competitive brothers could be. She suspected giving way to either of his younger brothers would be difficult for Jared. But, in Connor's case, it was likely he knew the right answer. He was the professional. She wasn't so sure about Josh, despite the expression of pure challenge on his face that seemed to say he knew he was right.

A muscle worked in Jared's jaw, causing her heart to beat double time. Men were so into proving themselves.

Jared motioned toward his brother. "Go ahead."

A wide smile spread across Josh's face.

"Good call," she mouthed, warmed that Jared had yielded.

"Assuming that he has it right. I read Connor the story

enough times when he was little. Hope Josh was listening, too." He scuffed the toe of his shoe against the edge of the area rug lifting it up and down. "We had this Bible storybook I used to read to them, mostly to Connor." He shuttered the look of vulnerability on his face as quickly as it appeared, making her want to know more about the real Jared Donnelly, the man who wasn't a celebrity motocross champion. The man who, as a teen, had read Bible stories to his younger brother. Not that she expected he'd be quick to share.

"Josh has it. The Singles Group wins," Tessa announced.

"Yes," Jared said under his breath. It had been hard to step back and let Josh have the day, both because of his years of thriving on competition and because of the little-brother, big-brother family dynamics. The few times Jared had been home the past few years, Josh had seemed to begrudge him his success and been ready to challenge him at any opportunity. Sadly, he'd been all too quick to rise to the challenge.

He stood and rubbed the back of his neck, certain Becca had caught on to some of that. And he didn't like it. He'd gotten comfortable living behind his world-champion facade. A facade that hid and helped him control things such as the rage he'd felt when his father had told eight-year-old Connor that Bible stories were for girls and taken the book, saying he was going to burn it with the trash. Jared had never seen the book again. With a role model like that, it was no wonder he'd decided it was in the world's best interest that he not become a parent.

"That was fun," Becca said.

"It was," Jared agreed, thinking that if he couldn't escape behind the facade, he needed to find a way to escape physically without being rude.

Becca smiled. "It would have been even if we'd lost."

He definitely needed to get somewhere he could collect his thoughts. He'd had too good of a time today, let down his guard with Becca and allowed himself to enjoy being with her without thinking of all the reasons he shouldn't, not the least of which were Brendon and Ari.

"I told you it would be fun." Emily walked up beside Jared. "And it was even more fun winning. Now we have to have a playoff. What do you say, Connor?"

"What do I say about what?"

"A playoff."

"No question. We need one," Eli said, as he and Jamie joined the group, followed by Josh and the woman he'd been partnered with for the game.

Jared's lungs constricted until he had trouble drawing a breath. They had him hemmed in. Through the window, he spotted his bike. That was what he needed, a rip across his property on Conifer Road.

"Are you okay?" Becca touched his arm.

"Looks like the asthma attacks he used to have when we were kids," Josh said.

Jared gritted his teeth. "I'm fine. I haven't had an asthma attack in twenty years." He drilled his gaze into his brother's to gauge whether he was trying to make him look weak in front of Becca and the others or was actually concerned. The lack of malice in Josh's eyes shamed Jared for thinking the worst of him.

"We've got coffee, cold drinks and brownies, courtesy of Jamie, in the hall kitchen," Emily said. "If that would help."

If one more person fussed over him, he was going to explode.

Connor cleared his throat. "And if we want to get to

those brownies, we need to wrap up here. Let's bow our heads in a closing prayer.

Thank you. Jared didn't know if Connor had done that for him or because he had an early day and wanted to get home. Connor was driving an elderly parishioner the fifty miles up to the Adirondack Medical Center in Saranac Lake where his wife was having early-morning surgery. It didn't matter. His intervention let Jared put things in perspective. The group wasn't hemming him in. Unlike the race crowds, they didn't want a piece of him. They were socializing. He could do this. He had to if he was going to pursue his dream.

"Amen," he said when Connor finished, his voice rising above the others. He hung back while the group filed out of the lounge.

Eli was waiting in the hall for him. "I wanted to catch you in case you weren't staying for food. I want to hear more about your racing school. Let me know when you're free. The morning math class I teach finishes at eleven. If we met at noon at the Camp Sonrise lodge, Drew Stacey could join us. He's the director and camp is in session. But he must get a lunch break. I'll call him tomorrow."

"I can do that. You can reach me at the parsonage."

"All right." Eli nodded toward the hall. "You should stay. I could be biased, but Jamie's brownies are as good as everyone says."

Socialize, Donnelly. As Connor had said, he needed to socialize, reach out to the locals and remind them he was one of them—for the project and for himself, too.

"You've talked me into it."

That and the fact that Becca was in the hall. He could talk with her about joining him and Eli and Drew to hear his plans for the school. That would be a better idea than getting together with her alone. Better and safer. Much safer. He wouldn't be putting himself in a situation like tonight where he might allow himself to be lulled into feeling comfortable with her and thinking there could be anything between them. He knew his reality. But Becca had a way of making him lose sight of it.

Becca poured a cup of coffee and glanced at the doorway of the church hall for the fifth time in two minutes. When she saw Jared walking in with Eli, she gave her full attention to adding cream and sugar to her drink. So, he hadn't left. She stirred her coffee, watching the white swirls of half-and-half disappear into the dark brown of the drink. They'd had such a good time competing together. Then afterward, he'd gone all weird.

"Becca."

She clanged the spoon against the side of the stoneware cup. "Jared. I thought you'd left."

"No." He hesitated and then flashed a tight smile. "I was talking with Eli. We're going to get together with Drew at the Camp Sonrise lodge so I can tell them more about my plans for the racing school."

She removed the spoon from the cup and placed it on a napkin next to the coffeemaker. The fun they'd had playing Bible trivia had totally pushed the motocross track from her mind. She'd just as soon it had stayed there.

"You can join us," he said.

"I'm working, but if you let me know which day, I could come over on my lunch break."

"Sure, Eli thought lunchtime would work best for Drew, too." He pulled out his cell phone. "I don't have you in my contacts."

Becca debated whether to give him her cell number or the house number and settled on the cell.

It would be easier to screen his call. At home, Brendon might pick up. And he could get Jared's number from the caller ID. She knew her son. If he had Jared's number, he'd use any excuse to call him, which wouldn't help her efforts to discourage his infatuation with motorcycles and Jared.

Jared finished punching in her number. "I'll give you a call as soon as I know what day is best for Drew."

"Monday, Wednesday or Friday is best for me. We bring the older kids down for swimming after lunch on those days. I can go out and join them at the beach when they get there."

"I remember."

She did, too. Becca's mind flashed back to running into Jared on the dock the other day. A small smile twitched her lips.

"Are you about ready to go?" Emily came up beside her. "Izzy has scout camp tomorrow, so I have to get her up and out early. We've been pretty lazy at our house about getting up mornings since school let out. All of us except Drew, of course."

Becca glanced from her half-full cup of coffee to Jared. *Not really.* Her kids were staying overnight at her ex-in-laws', so she didn't have to worry about getting them home and in bed. As much as she and Debbie and Ken clashed over many things, they were good about helping her with the kids.

"I guess." She should have driven herself, but Emily had offered to pick her up, and she'd liked the idea of not having to drive home alone to an empty house. Her house was fairly isolated, which she usually liked. But it wouldn't be for long if Jared built his racetrack. The meeting with him to find out more about his project couldn't come too soon. "Let me grab a brownie. I haven't had one."

"You'd better get one fast. There are only two left."

As Emily spoke, Jared reached around and picked up the plate of brownies from the table behind them, along with a couple of napkins. "I haven't had one either. Judging from how fast they went, they must be as good as Eli said."

"They definitely are," Emily said.

He gave Becca a napkin and offered her her choice of the two brownies.

She took one. "Since you've never had one before, I'll let you have the bigger one."

"You don't know what a sacrifice Becca is making," Emily teased.

Jared lifted the brownie to his lips and sunk his teeth into it. A look of pure delight spread across his face. "Are you sure you don't want to share half of the other one, too?"

"I'm sure," Becca said, biting into hers. "They're a million calories. But I'll deal with the aftermath."

He grinned. "And I know how. By running back and forth from the boulder in my meadow to your backyard to work them off. Don't say I didn't offer to help spare you."

"Shh," she said. "You're giving away my secrets. Emily thinks I can eat whatever I want and not gain an ounce."

Emily covered her ears. "No, don't tell me it's not true. Another illusion shattered."

Becca finished her coffee. "I'm ready to go if you still are."

"Yeah, we'd better. See you at the next meeting, Jared?" Emily asked.

"Probably. And I'll call you tomorrow, Becca, to let you know which day."

Emily raised an eyebrow as Becca said goodbye. As

soon as they were in the hall out of Jared's earshot, she grabbed Becca's arm. "Was that what I think it was?"

Becca shook her head. "I doubt it."

"That wasn't Jared Donnelly saying he was going to call you to get together?"

"Oh, that."

Emily's mouth curved up in a knowing smile.

"He and Eli and Drew are meeting so he can tell them more about his racetrack project, and he asked me if I wanted to come. I need to know a lot more before I cast my Zoning Board vote."

"That's all?"

"That's all. Now, will you stop turning every contact I have with the man into something more?"

Emily released an exaggerated sigh. "If I must." She pushed open the door, and they stepped outside. "You can't tell me you don't find him attractive."

"No, I can't. A woman would have to be dead to not find Jared Donnelly at least physically attractive."

"But Jared has other attractive qualities," Emily said. She unlocked her car and Becca opened the passenger side door.

"Yes. And unattractive ones, too, like he wants to build a motocross track in my backyard."

"Maybe it won't be as bad as you think. He keeps calling it a school, not a track."

"I'll find that out when we meet." Becca buckled her seat belt. But Emily made no move to start the car. "I thought you were in a hurry to get home."

"Yeah, I should be. But you two look really good together and made a great team at Bible trivia."

"You can stop anytime now."

"All right, but it's the first time since Matt left that

you seem interested in another man. As you said, you're not dead."

Leave it to Emily to use her own words against her. "Can we put an end to this conversation if I admit that, yes, I'm attracted to Jared? But there's no way I can pursue that attraction until the racetrack thing is settled." Becca gestured. "And probably not then, either. Not if I have to vote him down."

Chapter Six

Ari marched ahead of Becca into the Hazardtown Community Church hall, which served as the main room of The Kids' Place. "Mommy got her important call last night, so she's not going to have lunch with us today," she announced to Leanne, one of the other teachers.

"I have a meeting today at twelve-thirty at the camp lodge," Becca explained. "Zoning Board business. I don't expect it to take more than an hour. I can meet you at the lake when you bring the kids down for swimming lessons."

Ari put her backpack with her swimming stuff against the side wall in the space marked with red tape for her class. "Yeah, it's with Jared, the motorcycle-racing guy who's going to build a racetrack behind our house. Brendon says we'll probably get to go to the races for free because we're his friends."

"I don't know about that," Becca said.

"But Brendon said."

Becca thanked God daily that her kids were close, even when that closeness united them against her.

"Where is Brendon?" Leanne asked.

"He went to his friend Ian's. It's just me and Mommy today, except when she has to go to her meeting."

"Why don't you go down to your classroom," Leanne said. "And help Mrs. Hill finish setting up for the art project you're going to do today."

"Can I, Mom?"

"Sure." It bothered Becca that Ari always asked her permission before she did anything, even with people she knew well and was comfortable with. Her daughter's uncertainty reminded her too much of herself when she'd been Ari's age and her parents had temporarily separated. Becca had wanted to do everything right so both her parents would love her. Not that they hadn't. She hated to think her daughter was feeling the same insecurities she had. Her ex-husband's on-again, off-again use of his visitation rights didn't help. Never knowing whether she'd see her father when he'd promised confused Ari even more.

"Thanks," Becca said.

"No problem. I had an ulterior motive. Your meeting is about the proposed motocross track out your way?"

"Yes."

"Do you know where it's going to be built in relation to Camp Northern Lights?"

Becca hadn't thought about the Girl Scout camp on the parallel road west of Conifer Road. "No, I don't. When I looked at the preliminary plans Tom Hill showed me before the last Zoning Board meeting, it didn't strike me that Jared's property might border the camp property on that side."

"Can you find out for me? Both of my girls are scouts, and I'm the assistant leader for their troop. I hate to be against something that would bring jobs and business to the area, but I'm uncomfortable with a racetrack near a camp full of girls. You never know. The people it might draw. What might happen."

"I think a lot of people feel that way." Herself included, despite her efforts to be unbiased. "The public hearing next week should give us answers."

"I guess. I don't know if you remember the Donnelly brothers' father. Not a stellar citizen. Connor and Josh seem okay, but Jared hasn't been around here for years. What do we know about him?"

Leanne's changing from concerns about the track to concerns about Jared personally rankled Becca and compelled her to defend Jared and his project. "At the Singles Group meeting the other night, Jared stressed that the primary purpose of his project is a racing school for kids, based on tenets similar to those of the Boys & Girls Club organization."

"That's better and says something about Jared—that he wants to help kids. But I'd heard that there'd be regular professional races. No?"

Becca hesitated, as she remembered Jared doing when she'd asked the same question at Bible trivia. "Yes, there'll be racing. To bring in money for the kids' program and boost the local tourist trade."

Leanne shook her head. "We put up with that annual motorcycle rally for the sake of tourism. I'm not sure we need more of the same, even if it does bring in money."

Despite some of the stories her ex-father-in-law told, Becca hadn't seen anything herself or read anything in the *Times of Ti* that indicated the bikers attending the rally caused any more trouble than an equal number of other tourists would. There were just so many of them here at once.

"A motocross track wouldn't bring in anywhere near the number of people as the rally."

"Then it wouldn't even be worth it for the money."

She could argue that she'd meant all at one time, that the track could bring in that many people over the season. But why was she arguing at all? Leanne hadn't mentioned anything Becca didn't have concerns about herself. Instead of saying that, she was answering Leanne from Jared's perspective, from what he'd said the other evening at church, which made the issues seem less insurmountable. Her thoughts jumbled in her head. Leanne was an open-minded person, unlike her ex-in-laws. And if reasonable people were siding with the Sheriff and Debbie, it would be hard for her to oppose them. Her ex-in-laws would use that against her and, by association, against the kids. Besides she *was* concerned about having the track, school, whatever so close to her house. She'd go at lunchtime and hear Jared out about his project and be fair when it came up for vote by the Zoning Board. But she couldn't let her attraction to the man influence her thinking. Her kids came first and always would.

Jared glanced at his bike parked in the driveway of the parsonage. It had been too dark to ride his property last night when he'd left the church. He tapped the cardboard tube with the racetrack plans and survey map against his leg. And he'd spent the morning working on his presentation, so he hadn't gotten out today, either. The walk to the camp lodge would work the edge off his nervous energy, for now, and let him go over what he wanted to say to Eli and Drew one more time. He'd decided he might as well give them and Becca the presentation he'd give at the public hearing next week, with some additional information about the school that might interest the guys as youth workers and soften Becca's resistance.

At the sound of gravel crunching under tires, he lifted

his hand to shield his eyes from the midday sun and looked up the road toward the highway. A compact SUV slowed and stopped at the end of the parsonage driveway. Emily rolled down the window. "Hey, want a lift to the lodge?"

"No, thanks. Not to be rude, but I want the walk time to think."

Emily waved him off. "Don't sweat it. Drew and Eli aren't going to be a hard sell. Drew barely knows about it and he's already mapping out how your program can help his program. He's looking for ways to get some of our scholarship campers who come up from the city to keep coming when they're older."

"Good to know." But it wasn't Eli or Drew he expected to be his hard sell.

"See you up there." Emily started to close the window and stopped. "I just thought of something. If you want to do any kind of PR media blitz, I have time in my schedule." She paused. "You look confused. I'm a graphic artist. I worked for an advertising agency in Manhattan before I was married."

"I hadn't thought of that." A media campaign made sense. Get his information out like Connor had said.

"Well, think about it. I can give you a good deal."

"Money's not a problem."

"Good to know," she said echoing his earlier words. She finished rolling up the window and sped off.

"Hi."

Becca startled him.

"Hey, I didn't hear you walk up."

"I came across the yard from the church, but with all that gravel Emily was throwing, you might not have heard the whole day care walking up the road."

"I did notice the lead foot." He motioned her to the road and stepped around to the traffic side.

"That was nothing. We took the kids to ride the go-karts at Lake George. You would have thought she was racing a grand prix."

"All right. I need to put that girl on a bike."

Instead of the comeback he expected, he got silence. *Smart move, Donnelly.* There'd be plenty of opportunity to start a standoff about motorcycles when they got to the lodge. He didn't have to jump the gun and get into the conversation now.

"The trouble is, I can see Emily on a motorcycle."

"That's trouble?"

Becca frowned.

Why couldn't he keep his mouth shut? He usually picked his fights carefully, and the last thing he wanted to do was go into the meeting at the lodge at further odds with Becca.

"Have you always been into motorcycles, even when you were a kid?"

"You mean like Brendon's age?"

"Mmm-hmm. I don't remember you having a bike in high school."

"No, I didn't, not until the summer before my senior year. I signed up to take auto mechanics at Vo-Tech my senior year. I thought that was a way out of here. I used to work for Bert Miller." Bert Miller and anyone else he could to have extra money to give his mom. But he didn't need to tell Becca that. Considering her family, she'd have no way to relate to his dysfunctional one. "He had an old beat-up dirt bike in his garden shed. I asked if I could have it to fix up as part of my pay. He said I could have it and offered to help me work on it."

"That was nice of him."

"Yeah." It had been and Bert had never said why he'd done it. Nor did Jared know why Bert had given him the property on Conifer Road or helped out Josh and Connor, other than what his grandmother had said about him and his dad being friends at one time. Since it seemed to involve his father, he'd be better off not knowing.

"That was the bike Tessa was talking about."

"Right."

"When you got it running, you decided to race rather than become a mechanic?"

The inflection in her tone said her choice wouldn't have been racing. "No, it didn't even occur to me. But it turned out to have been a lot more lucrative choice."

"Then how?"

"Bert saw me tooling around the fields before I got the bike on the road, and said I was a natural. Apparently, he'd done some racing when he was in his twenties. He still had racing contacts and got me into some local amateur races. After I left Paradox Lake, I supported myself and my bike working as a mechanic until I could race full-time."

"Bert Miller was a motorcycle racer?"

The kaleidoscope of expressions crossing Becca's face said she was trying to reconcile Bert Miller the local bank manager with Bert Miller the bike racer.

"Yep, it happens even in the best families."

Becca stopped and put her hands on her hips. "That wasn't necessary. I didn't mean it to sound that way. I know nothing about motocross or any other kind of racing, except what I've read in Brendon's magazines."

"That's why I asked you to come to this meeting. I want to show you and Eli and Drew the reasons Paradox Lake is the right place for my motocross school. I need people like you three with me."

"I'll keep an open mind."

"That's all I can ask."

But, Jared thought as they walked up the pine steps to the Camp Sonrise lodge, would that be enough to get her behind his plans? His thoughts ran to the other night, how much fun he'd had with her, how well they'd worked together as a team. Against his better judgment, he wondered if her open mind applied to him, too.

"Any more questions?"

Watching Jared across the table, Becca couldn't help comparing him with Brendon when he was finishing up an explanation of some accomplishment at school or at soccer practice and waiting for her approval. His energy. The way he perched on the edge of his chair. His excited gestures. No one could question that Jared was one hundred and ten percent behind launching his motocross school.

"I'm good," Eli said. "I can see your program being really valuable for some of the students I advise at the high school. It could have been for me after we lost my Dad when I was fourteen. Something like this might have pulled me out of the spiral of trouble that nearly sucked me to the bottom before I joined the Air Force out of high school."

"Got my answers," Drew said. "I'll work up some ideas for integrating your program with my senior camper program and our youth group activities and get back to you."

Jared's gaze went to Becca, and she wanted to meet it with the same enthusiasm as Eli and Drew. "I agree with Eli and Drew about the premise of the school."

"But there's something you're not satisfied with," he said giving her an opening to voice her unresolved issues.

Several somethings. "I don't have any more questions." She'd answer him professionally without letting her personal concerns color her words. "I have some advice for the public hearing."

He crossed his arms. "I'm listening."

She would not let him intimidate her. "Get the updated traffic studies before the meeting. I know people are concerned about traffic and the possibility of a roundabout. You need to come up with a way to reassure some people that the professional races won't bring in what they may see as an undesirable element. Among other things, I know people are concerned about the proximity to the Girl Scout camp."

Jared uncrossed his arms and she filled her empty lungs.

He leaned forward on his elbows. "I'm glad you brought up the camp. I hadn't thought of it. I'll talk to the scouting council. The racing program is for girls, too. As for the undesirable element, Emily suggested a media campaign."

"Good idea. She does excellent work."

Drew acknowledged Becca's recognition of his wife's ability with a nod. "She's done a lot of national ad campaigns."

Uncertainty waved over Becca. Jared using Emily could work against Becca if she decided she couldn't support the project.

"These are good." He tapped a note into his cell phone. "Anything else?"

She hated to extinguish the expectation that lit his eyes again. "I disagree about the program being open to kids younger than twelve or thirteen."

"You're a teacher," Jared said. "You know what some kids are into by the time they're in middle school."

Becca did know, but her kids wouldn't. She wouldn't let them.

When she didn't say anything, he continued, "I want to get the kids involved before they even start thinking about getting into in trouble."

"Racing is dangerous." She made the only argument she had in her arsenal. The only one besides it scared her, which carried zero weight against any of Jared's points.

"More dangerous than drinking or drugs or vandalism?"

Eli and Drew had faded into the background. This was between her and Jared.

"No, and don't think I have my head buried in the sand. I know what goes on." She did. But she was a good parent. A Christian parent.

Eli snapped shut the notebook he'd used for notes, bringing him and Drew back into the picture.

Eli's mother, a single mother, had been a good parent. From what Jared's grandmother had shared with her, Jared's mother, a single mother for all intents and purposes, was a good mother. Both had raised their children in the church. Pain split her chest. They probably prayed for God to watch over their boys as hard as she prayed the same prayer for Brendon and Ari. Obviously, the Lord's plan for her was to be a single parent. But in her now-broken plans for her life and having kids, that had never even been a blip on the radar.

"Then you know how young some of them are. Part of the problem is the lack of activities, outside of school, for the kids as they get older. And for kids like I was who aren't involved in school."

He was so earnest. Her resolve softened. She was thinking in terms of Brendon, not other kids it could help.

"The program will be different for the younger children, with scaled-down, less powerful bikes."

A knock sounded on the lodge door. "Hi," Leanne said. "We're here with the kids for swim lessons."

"Which means I have to get back to work," Drew said.

"Me, too," Becca said.

"Think about it. I'll send you the curriculum. Connor has your email?"

"Yes, and I will think about it. Everything we talked about."

Becca was still thinking about Jared and his plans when she stepped out of the church hall into the humid evening air. Despite her having left the front windows cracked open, the air in the car was even more stifling than it was outside. She turned the key and got nothing but a clicking sound. It couldn't be the battery. She'd just had it replaced. Becca tried again as the thick hot air threatened to suffocate her.

She pulled the hood lever, threw open the door and walked to the front of the car. A quick check showed the battery cables were tightly connected. No belts looked to be broken or missing. She grabbed her phone from her pocket and punched in the number for Tom Hill's garage. As the phone rang, she prayed it wasn't anything major. The car needed to make it until October. That's when the home equity loan Matt had given her along with the house would be paid off, and she could afford to buy a new one.

The line went dead before anyone answered, typical of the spotty cell phone coverage in the mountains. She walked to the different corners of the parking lot to see if she could pick up a connection, stopping when she heard the crescendoing sound of a motorcycle turning off the highway onto Hazard Cove Road. Becca looked around at the tall pines that lined the parking lot and stiffened. She was alone. The church hall blocked any view Connor might have of her from the parsonage, if he were home. She breathed in and out and shook her hands. She shouldn't let Leanne's comments this morning get to her. This was the parking lot of the church. She walked back to the car. *Duh!* She could call Tom from the phone inside.

As the sound of the bike continued to grow louder, she glanced toward the road, expecting to see it fly by toward the lake. Instead, the rider slowed and turned into the parking lot. Her heart raced. A gray face guard obscured his features. Becca judged the distance to the hall door and how long it would take her to grab the keys from the car and unlock it. She pushed her hair back from her eyes and stared hard at the rider. It was Jared. Relief and embarrassment pooled inside her. If she'd looked at the motorcycle, she would have recognized the distinctive green color. The heat, the car and Leanne's words had set her nerves on edge.

He slowed to a stop next to her, shut off the engine and removed his helmet. "Hi. What's the problem?" He lifted his chin toward the open hood of her car.

A bubble of giddiness rose inside her. Her knight in shining chrome.

"I don't know. It won't start. The battery is new, and I checked the battery cables to make sure they weren't loose."

"I'll take a look. The keys?"

"In the car," she said, waiting for the look of disapproval she would have gotten from her ex-husband. "I should have grabbed them."

Jared shrugged as if it were no big deal. He lowered the kickstand of his bike and swung his denim-clad leg over and off. Becca stood by the side of the car while he folded himself in and moved the seat back. He turned the key with the same result she'd gotten.

He turned it back. "Sounds like the alternator went."

"When you drove up, I was going inside to call Hill's Garage. Guess I'd better."

"I can replace it. I'd have to go into Ticonderoga to get the part, so it wouldn't be until tomorrow."

"Thanks, but you don't have to. I usually take it to Tom's."

"I know I don't have to, but you'd be doing me a favor to let me."

Was Jared flirting with her? Her heart thumped. It had been so long since she'd been in a situation where that would happen that she was unsure if he was or if it was wishful thinking on her part.

"I have lots of time on my hands. I've got my bikes in top running order, my truck tuned, Connor and Josh's cars tuned, new brakes on Grandma's car and a new catalytic converter installed on Harry's car."

"Tom had better watch it or he'll have no customers left."

"That's not a problem for the next few days. He and his family are on vacation until Tuesday. The garage is closed through Wednesday. I called him there with a zoning question and got that message. Connor filled me in on the vacation part."

"Oh." She really had no choice but to let Jared fix her car, unless she wanted to have the car towed to a garage in Ticonderoga. That might cost as much as the repair. "Okay. I'll pay, of course."

"Of course. I think a home-cooked meal would be a fair price, parts included."

His offer was tempting. She'd need to pay him cash.

Tom accepted credit cards, so if the repair was expensive, she could pay it off over a couple of months. But she had the money she was putting away to fill the oil tank at the house in the fall before winter set in.

"I wouldn't feel right." Which was true. She'd feel indebted to him. An uneasy thought passed through her mind. Was that his point? To make her feel indebted so she'd be more inclined to vote for his racing project?

"It's no big deal." A trace of impatience laced his words. "You need your car running. I need some good cooking. I think I'm close to wearing out my welcome at Grandma's."

"I doubt Edna would ever get tired of having you stop in for dinner." The thought of the love and admiration Becca knew Edna had for her grandson blotted out any idea she may have had earlier that Jared was trying to buy her vote. "Besides, how do you know my cooking is good?"

"Anything is better than what Connor and I have been making."

Becca laughed. "Should we start a fund to send Pastor to culinary arts classes at North Country Community College in Saranac?"

"It wouldn't be a bad idea. Neither would taking me up on my offer."

"You're persistent, if nothing else."

"I'm lots of other things."

Had his voice dropped or was it her imagination? "All right. I accept your offer to fix my car. But I pay for the parts. The dinner is for your labor."

"Deal, for my fixing your car and giving you and the kids a lift home tonight." He looked around as if he'd just noticed Ari and Brendon weren't there. "Are they inside? I'll go get my truck."

Becca ignored that Jared thought she'd leave a five-and nine-year-old inside by themselves. He wasn't a parent. His father may have left him alone, or even alone watching his brothers when he was Brendon's age. That could be part of the reason he didn't understand her opposition to having the racing school include young kids. In high school, Jared had seemed old for his age to her. Maybe he always had been—and responsible. A lot of kids weren't.

"No, Brendon spent the day at the Hazards' with Ian, and when Anne Hazard picked up her daughter Sophia from swimming lessons at the lake, she invited Ari to come and stay for dinner."

"So you're free to pay me for the car work in advance."

Becca's heart flip-flopped. She and Jared alone at her house tonight. "Sorry, not if you want something home cooked. I already called the deli at the Paradox General Store and ordered a sub to pick up on my way home." Part of her was glad for the excuse. She needed to prepare for having him over. The other part shouted, *You could have the sub for lunch tomorrow.*

"What about tomorrow, when I bring your car back?"

Tomorrow was Saturday. The kids would be there. She'd have time to make a nice dinner for all of them. "Tomorrow's good."

"Great. I'll get you home, then."

She eyed his motorcycle. It had a second helmet fastened on the back.

"I've never ridden on a motorcycle before." Her heart rate picked up and her hands went clammy.

"I can get my truck."

She didn't want Jared to know she was afraid. Becca breathed a cleansing breath. She could do this. "No."

She cleared her throat. "There has to be a first time for everything."

"That's the spirit." He unfastened the helmet and handed it to her.

She pulled it on and fastened the chin strap.

Jared reached over, his forefinger gently stroking her chin as he checked the fit of the strap. She steeled herself against reacting, but her shiver gave her away. His eyes darkened.

"The fit's good." He put on his helmet and positioned himself on the bike. "Climb on behind me."

She took a moment to decide whether she could do that without touching him. *No way.* She placed her hands on his forearm and swung her leg over, uncertain what to do with her hands now that she was seated.

His helmet shook with what might have been a laugh. He flipped up the face guard and turned around. "Sorry, I don't have grip bars. You're going to have to put your arms around me."

He didn't sound sorry to her at all. Becca reached around.

"Ready?" He started the motor.

As ready as she could be.

He drove slowly across the parking lot, his clean masculine scent filling her breathing space. Her fingertips gripped his rock-hard abs, sending a shiver through her that had nothing to do with the wind whipping them. As he sped up on the highway, she leaned against him and gave in to the free feeling of throwing her fears and cares to that wind—if only for a moment.

She'd worry later about how she was going to keep a level mind and not let her awakening feelings for Jared color her decision when his racing-school project came up for vote before the Zoning Board.

Chapter Seven

"Mom, it's not fair." Brendon slammed into the kitchen ahead of Ari.

Becca crumpled the wrapping from her sub and tossed it in the kitchen trash can. "What's not fair?"

Her son shoved the smart hone her ex-husband had given him—against her wishes—at her.

"This," he spat, pointing at a text from his father.

"Watch your tone." Whatever she might think or feel about Matt, he was Brendon's father.

"But Dad says we have to come to his house this weekend. His work is having a picnic or something that he wants to take us to."

To show off what a good family man he is. Becca regretted the thought, but it was the way she saw things.

"I'm all signed up to go to the fishing derby on Sunday with Ian and Mr. Hazard. Remember, last year, I almost won. Ian and I have been practicing our technique."

Becca closed her eyes for a moment. She knew how much Brendon had been looking forward to the derby and wished she could say no to Matt. But he was supposed to have the kids two weekends a month and hadn't had them in a couple of months. He'd been "too busy with work."

"Can't you call Dad and tell him we'll come next weekend?" Brendon begged.

She wished she could. Matt had a reason for them coming this weekend, although he should have given them more than a day's notice. Who knew when he would want them to come again? She wavered, remembering how much she'd hated the disruption of going to Albany to stay with her mother when her parents had separated temporarily. She'd never felt comfortable in the city or in the apartment her mother had shared with a friend from high school. And her parents had argued about it constantly, with her dad trying to explain to Mom how upsetting the visits had been for her. She'd often wondered how her parents had overcome their differences and put their marriage back together. But she'd never asked, even when her own marriage had been falling apart. She hadn't wanted to revisit that part of her childhood.

"No. It'll be fun. You like picnics. There'll probably be games and prizes. Maybe you'll win one."

"It wouldn't be the same as winning the fishing derby."

"Maybe not, but your father wants you to come. He hasn't seen you and Ari in a while."

"Fine. Dad said Grandma and Grandpa will pick us up at nine tomorrow morning." Brendon stomped off to his room.

"Mommy," Ari said. "Can I ride with you tomorrow, instead of Grandma and Grandpa?"

Becca squatted to Ari's level. "What do you mean, honey?"

"I don't like riding with Grandpa. He puts the radio on too loud. Grandma says he needs to get a hearing aid."

"I'm not going," Becca said, Ari's subdued tone pulling at her heartstrings. Since Matt had left before her daughter had been born, Ari had never had the opportunity to form a real relationship with her father.

"But Brendon's text says it's a family picnic. You're family."

"I'm your family, but not Daddy and Crystal's family. It's Daddy's family picnic."

Ari shook her head. "I don't understand."

Becca wrapped her arms around her daughter. She didn't understand, either. She'd always tried to do everything right. How had her life turned out so unsettled? More than that, how could she make it more stable? The rev of a motorcycle on the highway sounded in the distance. Certainly not by inviting Jared Donnelly into their lives.

Jared wiped his hands on his jeans. Becca's car had had a whole lot more wrong with it than the faulty alternator. He let the hood drop shut. She'd been putting her and her kids' lives in danger driving it. But no longer. He'd taken care of all of it, including four new all-weather tires. Given his bad memories of the heaps his mother had had to drive because there'd been no money to repair them or buy anything better, his conscience would let him do no less.

"All fixed?" Connor joined him in the parsonage garage.

"Yep, all fixed, tuned and ready to go. Becca shouldn't have any more problems with it for a while."

"You did more than replace the alternator."

"Some."

Connor's eyes narrowed.

"Okay, a lot more."

"What are you going to tell Becca?"

"Nothing, except for the tires. I'm sure she's going to notice them."

"And, if I know Becca, which I do, she's going to insist on paying for them with money she may not have."

Jared didn't know if he was more irritated with Connor's familiarity with Becca or with himself for wanting to hide the work he'd done on her car from her.

"Tom Hill will notice, too, the next time she takes her car in for maintenance."

He could have slapped himself in the head. He hadn't thought of that. All he'd thought of was how dangerous her car was for her to be driving and how he could fix it. "I could talk with Tom."

"Talk with Tom Hill, the chairperson of the Zoning Board, about doing how many hundreds of dollars of repairs free for another member of the board the week before the public hearing on your racing-school project."

"I've really dug myself in."

"That you have, not to mention the lying factor if you don't tell her."

"I wasn't planning to lie, just not tell her. What she doesn't see doesn't hurt. The car was a mechanical wreck."

"Semantics. A lie of omission is still a lie in the eyes of our Lord."

Connor's pointed response set off his already uneasy conscience. "Okay, so I don't tell her and talk with Tom and it looks like I'm bribing a board member, or I do tell her and it looks like I'm bribing a board member."

"You've got it." Connor slapped him on the back. "Better start saying some prayers."

"Knock it off. You know as well as I do, receiving God's forgiveness is going to be lot easier than getting Becca to forgive me."

"I have no doubts about that. Enjoy your dinner."

Jared chucked an oily rag at his brother's retreating figure.

Half an hour later Jared had showered, dressed and was ready to face Becca. He'd put on his "feel good" shirt, a blue polo his mother had given him several years ago that had been washed to a comfortable softness. Mom had said she'd bought it on impulse because it was the same color as his eyes and reminded her of a shirt he'd loved when he was little. He didn't remember that shirt but, for whatever reason, he'd always felt he could handle anything he ran up against when he wore the one his mother had given him.

As he drove Becca's car by the Paradox Lake General store, he tapped the brake and thought about pulling in to see if they had any cut flowers today. He could get her a bouquet. Or something for the kids. A book or kite or some treat. He lifted his foot from the brake. She'd probably see the flowers as him spending even more money on her and anything for the kids as a not-so-subtle bribe to soften her up so she wouldn't be too mad about the car. *The kids.* It struck him that she couldn't get too angry at him about the car if the kids were around. The weight on his chest crumbled. He pushed the On button and the car radio came to life with Resurrection Light, a Christian rock band with roots in Ticonderoga, singing one of their early songs about conquering mountains. Jared joined in. He'd handle it. Tonight would be fine.

Becca touched up her makeup and changed out of the T-shirt she'd worn while she'd cooked. She pulled on a brilliant blue cotton top with a scoop neckline and cap sleeves and smoothed it over her rolled-cuff denim shorts. Standing in front of the mirror, she released her hair from the band that held it knotted on top of her head and watched it tumble down around her shoulders.

"Not bad," she said to her reflection. "Not bad at all for a thirty-four-year-old history teacher and mother of two."

After running a brush through her hair, she went downstairs to the kitchen. The pot roast and veggies simmering in the cast-iron pan in the oven filled the room with a mouth-watering aroma. She could only hope it would taste as good as it smelled. Cooking wasn't something she spent much time doing. She and the kids ate simple and healthy. But Jared seemed like a meat-and-potatoes kind of guy. She checked the clock over the sink and scanned the room. He'd be here in fifteen minutes. The strawberry-rhubarb pie she'd baked this afternoon was cooling on the counter. Edna Stowe had given her the recipe after she'd complimented her on her pie at a church dinner. Mint iced tea was cooling in the refrigerator, and she'd picked up a variety pack of one-cup coffees in case Jared preferred coffee.

Nothing to do but wait. She sat in one of the tall-back kitchen chairs and crossed and uncrossed her legs until the sound of a car pulling in her driveway saved her. She jumped up and opened the oven door so it wouldn't look as if she'd just been sitting there waiting for him. At his firm knock she closed the oven, turned to the door with a smile and waved at the window for him to come in.

He pushed open the door. "Hi. Something smells good."

"Pot roast with potatoes, onions, carrots and green peppers."

"One of my favorites."

"Good," she said, pleased that she'd pegged him right. "Everything should be done. Do you want something to drink while I get the food on the table? I have mint iced tea or coffee."

"I'll take tea."

She got the pitcher from the refrigerator, filled the glasses on the table and motioned him to sit.

He eyed the table and pointed at the two settings. "The kids aren't eating with us?"

Becca lifted the roast from the oven and placed it on the top of the stove. Something in his voice made it sound as though he'd prefer they were here.

"They've gone to their father's for the weekend." She moved the roast to a serving platter, sliced it and arranged the vegetables around the meat.

Jared ran his finger down and up the condensation on the side of his tea glass as she carried the platter to the table.

Did he think she'd purposely arranged for them to be alone? This dinner had been his idea. "When we talked yesterday, I didn't know Matt wanted the kids this weekend."

"He didn't give you much notice."

"No. He texted Brendon late yesterday afternoon when Brendon was at Ian's."

She placed the platter in the center of the table and took the seat across from him, her hands crossed in her lap and head bowed for her silent grace.

"Dear Lord."

His deep voice startled her.

"Thank You for this food and for the dinner company. Amen."

"Amen." Becca's surprise turned to pleasure. Pleasure in knowing he still practiced his faith. She'd gotten mixed signals from him. He'd come to the Bible trivia but hadn't been to services at Hazardtown Community

Church since he'd returned. It seemed unlikely he'd attend services at a church other than his brother's. But as Leanne had said, what did they know about him?

"Guests first." She pushed the serving platter a couple of inches closer to Jared and watched him take a healthy helping. "Leave some room for the strawberry-rhubarb pie I made for dessert." The minute the words were out she wanted to take them back. That was something she'd say to the kids. She really needed to get out and socialize without them more. Maybe she could if Matt continued to take them on his weekends. Guilt pricked her. She hadn't noticed any lack of adult time until Jared had returned to town.

"Strawberry-rhubarb pie. No way would I miss out on that." He rotated the platter so she could reach the serving fork.

"It's your grandmother's recipe."

"You certainly know the way to a man's heart."

She caught a faint glaze of pink on Jared's cheeks before he bowed his head and gave his dinner one hundred percent of his concentration. The mouthful of food Becca had just swallowed stuck in her throat. Evidently, she wasn't the only one blurting first thoughts.

After an interminably long moment of silence, Jared spoke. "Everything is delicious. With the pie thrown in, I might have to do some more work on your car so I'm not overcharging you."

"Let's not go overboard," she said, kind of wishing he'd skipped the explanation and wondering about the shadow that crossed his face.

They talked until it was time for dessert, carefully ignoring any mention of Jared's racing project.

"Still have room for that pie?" Becca asked after Jared had finished a second helping and declared himself done.

"Definitely."

Becca rose, went to the cupboard and took down two dessert plates. As she was carrying their pieces of pie to the table, someone knocked at the kitchen door. She and Jared looked toward the sound.

A woman smiled at her through the door window. Charlotte Russell, one of the biggest gossips in Paradox Lake. Charlotte wasn't a mean person. It was more like she couldn't help sharing everyone else's business.

Becca placed the desserts on the table and went to the door.

"I didn't know you had company," Charlotte said when Becca let her in. "I only saw your car in the driveway."

Charlotte's eyes gleamed when she recognized Jared, and Becca's heart sank.

"Jared Donnelly," Charlotte said. "Wait until I tell my guys I met you. They're big fans of yours."

Jared stood and Becca introduced him to Charlotte.

"Sorry to interrupt your dinner," Charlotte said. "But I was on my way home from Ticonderoga and thought I'd stop in and pick up the Walk Out Hunger registration forms Debbie said she'd type and print out for Sunday school tomorrow. She said she'd drop them off with you before they left for the weekend."

"She didn't give me anything when she and Ken picked up the kids this morning."

The gleam in Charlotte's eyes brightened. Debbie must not have said anything to her about taking the kids with them to Connecticut. But now *she* had.

Charlotte released an exaggerated sigh. "I'll have to do them myself. We want to give the Sunday school kids a couple of weeks to sign up sponsors for the walk. Again, sorry for interrupting. See you tomorrow at church."

"Right." Becca closed the door behind Charlotte and

squeezed her eyes shut to dispel the feeling of impending doom.

"What?" Jared asked when Becca turned back toward him.

"Nothing." She sat back down and cut through her pie with her fork.

"No, it's something." His tone demanded an explanation.

She lowered her fork to the plate. "Charlotte is a gossip. She can't seem to help herself. By church time tomorrow, everyone in a twenty-mile radius will know you *secretly* had dinner with me at my house tonight while Brendon and Ari were in Connecticut with their father."

"What do you mean secretly?"

"You didn't drive your truck or bike here. Or you hid your vehicle so no one would know you're here." She gritted her teeth, remembering Ken's insinuations the day she and Jared had run into each other in the meadow. How Ken had accused Jared of concealing his vehicle so no one would know he was at her house when the kids were gone.

"We're two adults having dinner together. It's not like we're doing something illegal. If anyone says something, tell them I fixed your car and drove it over when I finished. Which I did. Not that it's anyone else's business."

"With the public hearing on your project next week and my being on the Zoning Board, that explanation isn't any better, even though it's the truth."

Jared rocked back in his chair. "Connor said the same thing about me fixing your car and that I needed to be up-front with you."

"What do you mean?" Dread bulldozed over her. "Up-front about what?"

"Your car. There was a lot more wrong with it than

the alternator." He tapped the table with his fingertips. "I kind of fixed everything and bought four new all-weather tires."

"And you weren't going to tell me?" She was too drained to express her full anger. "If that gets out, it's even worse. I'd have to recuse myself from the Zoning Board vote."

"Would that be so bad?"

"Maybe not." If she weren't in on the board vote, she wouldn't have to be evenhanded about the racetrack. She could look at the project as an individual citizen and consider only how it would affect her and her family. Not as a public official who might have to ignore her personal feelings for the benefit of the community. "But I'd still have to put up with the gossip."

"Don't let what other people think or say bother you. I don't." His body tightened. "But I've had more practice hardening myself against caring. You wouldn't believe some of the lies published about me."

Looking back at the weeks after Matt had first left her and she'd found out she was expecting Ari, Becca wasn't so sure he'd had that much more practice. And he was talking about the media, people he didn't know.

"It's not other people. It's the Sheriff and Debbie. They'd like Matt and his new wife to have custody of the kids." She loathed the way her voice cracked.

"They can't make that happen just because it's what they want." He got up and came around the table to her. Taking her hand, he urged her to her feet.

"No, not even the Sheriff can force the Family Court. But he can make things hard on the kids and me."

Jared wrapped his arms around her and she made no move to stop him.

"Matt might be able to get joint custody. He…I…" She

didn't want to talk about her problems. She wanted one moment to forget them, to lean on someone else, on Jared. To feel his warmth and strength. "You don't want to hear about it." When she'd collected herself, she slipped from his loose embrace. "I'd better drive you home."

"You're in no shape to drive. I'll call Connor."

"All right. And, to avoid any appearance of impropriety, I'll pay you back for the car repairs in cash."

His lips thinned. He'd better not tell her again that he could afford to take care of it for her. She took care of herself and her own.

"Okay. Your choice." His expression shouted anything but agreement.

She mustered what strength she had left. "One more thing. We need to avoid contact, at least until after the Zoning Board makes its decision on your project." Longer than that if she knew what was good for her.

His eyes darkened with anger. Or was it disappointment?

She bit her lip. Any relationship with Jared, even friendship, had too many complications.

That was it? Nice knowing you, but I don't want to be seen with you. Jared strode up Conifer Road toward the highway. No way could he stand still and wait for Connor. He slowed his pace as he got close to the intersection. Why should he expect any different? It didn't matter what he'd done with his life, in Paradox Lake he'd always be Jerry Donnelly's kid. And Becca Norton would always be one of the untouchables to him.

Beep! Connor turned his car on to Conifer Road and stopped next to Jared, who yanked the passenger-side door open. "Did you think I wouldn't see you?

"I'm not going to even ask." Connor did a U-turn and headed back home.

"Good."

They rode in silence to the parsonage. Connor pulled into the garage, and Jared reached for the door handle as his brother turned off the car. Maybe he'd take his bike out and blow off some steam. "Thanks for the lift. I'll catch you later. I'm going to go for a ride."

Connor looked out the garage door. "Those clouds are nasty looking."

"I know what I'm doing, little brother."

Connor mumbled what sounded like, "I hope so."

He turned his back on Connor and the car and tramped across the garage to his bike. He was used to making decisions and acting on them. Since he'd come back, everyone seemed to have directions and second guesses for him. Jared fired up the bike and gunned the engine, letting the vibration ease his tension. As the engine wound down, Jared saw a flash of lightning, followed by an almost immediate crash of thunder. He cranked off the motor and swung off. One more corner heard from.

He swung open the door from the garage to the house. Resurrection Light was blaring from Connor's office, almost drowning out the sound of the house phone ringing. "Connor," Jared shouted, figuring the call was for him. It stopped ringing as Jared picked up the receiver. He punched in the parsonage's phone number and voice mail code.

"You have one new message. Press One for new messages." He hit One.

"First new message, received Saturday at nine-fifty-nine p.m. 'Jared Donnelly, watch the channel 44 news tonight and see what people really think about your motocross racetrack.'"

"What's up?" Connor bounded down the stairs. "I was fine-tuning tomorrow's sermon."

"The phone was ringing. I figured it was for you."

"And it wasn't?"

"No, it was for me. Someone left a message telling me to watch the channel 44 news."

"You going to?"

"Might as well. Want to join me?"

"Sure."

Jared settled back in the recliner and turned on the TV.

"Now to our on-the-spot reporter Kelly Keene with a report filmed in Schroon Lake this afternoon."

"Kelly Keene, talking to some of the participants in what appears to be a spontaneous protest against international motocross champion and Paradox Lake native, Jared Donnelly's plans to build a motocross racetrack on Conifer Road near Paradox Lake in the Town of Schroon."

"Motocross school," Jared automatically corrected.

The camera panned to twenty or more people walking up and down Route 9 carrying signs with an X-ed out picture of him crossing the finish line of his final race before he'd retired.

"Did you know anything about this?" He slammed the footrest of the chair down and paced the length of the room.

Connor frowned. "Like I wouldn't have told you? The reporter said spontaneous."

"People just individually showed up at the same time with matching signs?"

Connor shushed him. "Sit down and listen. Maybe we'll find out."

Since when had his baby brother become the one to

keep him in check? He lowered himself back into the chair and focused on the TV.

The reporter tilted her microphone toward a man walking by with a sign. "Sir, can I ask you a few questions?" The man nodded. "What brought you out here today?"

"A friend called and said he was driving by and saw a woman here in front of the school with signs organizing the protest. I came right down. I've been looking for way to fight this thing. We don't need the kind of people a racetrack would draw, especially right near the Girl Scout camp."

"Right, people like me," Jared said. "He sounds just like Sheriff Norton. Norton probably set it all up before he took off for the weekend."

"Jared," Connor admonished. "You don't know that. A lot of people have questions about your project. That's what the public hearing Tuesday is for. To answer those questions.

He glared at Connor. "People with signs X-ing me out are not asking questions."

"You're making it too personal."

"It is personal. The project is my personal calling. It's my face X-ed out on those posters. You can't get more personal than that." He clamped his mouth shut. He'd said too much.

Connor simply raised an eyebrow.

"Thank you, sir," the TV reporter said before leaving him to talk briefly with a couple other protesters.

The camera faded to the newsroom. "That was Kelly Keene from Schroon Lake earlier this afternoon," the news anchor said. "There will be a public hearing on Jared Donnelly's motocross track Tuesday night at seven at the Schroon Town Hall."

Jared flicked off the TV. "I'm not the only one making it personal. It's not my track—now they have me saying it. My racing school," he corrected himself. "It's for the kids and for the town. Not for me. I could build it anywhere. I wanted to build it here, where I started."

Maybe he was crazy to think people would accept him enough to let him bring some good back to the place where his father had done so much harm, caused his family and others so much pain. The Donnelly name hadn't always been synonymous with loser. His father had done that, topping it off with his disappearance. He'd been last seen staggering out of a bar in Saranac Lake, leaving his old truck in the parking lot. Neither the police nor the private detective Jared had hired for his mother had found a trace of him after that. She'd been forced to have his father declared dead so she could sell the family home to buy a condo in the community where her sister lived.

Was he wrong to want to right things for Josh and Connor, for his mother if she ever wanted to come back, for himself?

Jared tossed the remote on the table. "You're the one person I know who might understand this. I want to give back some of my success, and nobody wants it."

"Yeah, I can relate. But stay calm. Everyone isn't against you. You've got the support of Eli and Drew, the Hazards, Gram and Harry, GreenSpaces Engineering. That's some influential people."

But that wasn't enough. He needed more. *Becca*, a voice in his head said, which was ridiculous. His project didn't need Becca's support. She was one vote on the Zoning Board. Nothing more. He needed the community to embrace his project. Or, remembering how Becca had felt in his arms, his inner voice asked, *Is it Becca's embrace you need?*

He shut out the voice.

Chapter Eight

Becca would have thrown the cell phone across the room if she hadn't owed Jared so much for the car repairs and could afford to replace it. She calmed herself and reread the Sheriff's text.

I'm counting on you tonight.

Innocent enough taken out of context. Not so innocent given that it was Tuesday and Brendon and Ari were still in Connecticut with Matt, his wife and his parents.

The phone rang. *It had better not be him with more veiled threats.* She checked the caller ID and was relieved to see it was Emily.

"Hi." She sat on the edge of her bed.

"Hey. Did you want to ride with us to the meeting? It's no problem for us to drop your kids off at the Nortons' if they're watching them there."

"No."

After a moment Emily said, "I'm confused. No, you don't want a ride? No, we wouldn't have to drop off the kids?"

"Oh, Emily." She stopped herself. *No!* She needed to

tell someone. "I'm so angry and disgusted and a little scared. The kids are still in Connecticut. Debbie called Sunday night when they should have already been back and said the kids were having such a good time that they were staying a few more days, maybe the whole week. Matt didn't even have the decency to call himself. And Debbie reminded me, coached by the Sheriff, I'm sure, that our custody agreement gives Matt the kids for a month every summer. He's never taken that time before."

"Have you talked with the kids?"

"No, I haven't. Much as I disagreed about Brendon having a cell phone, I was glad he had it this weekend. Except, when I called it went directly to voice mail, and he hasn't answered any of my texts. Either he forgot his charger or his father or grandfather has turned it off."

"Are we a little paranoid?"

"Probably. I just have a bad feeling."

"That feeling didn't happen to start with Saturday dinner by any chance? Maybe the reason you didn't come to Sunday services?"

Becca groaned. "What did Charlotte say?" She'd gone to services at her parents' old church in Schroon Lake rather than at Hazardtown Community Church.

"Not too much, for Charlotte. She thinks you make a cute couple and said it's like *Romeo and Juliet*, with Jared's racing school and your family being set against it."

"More than you know," Becca said just out of Emily's hearing range.

"Pardon?"

"Nothing. I wish people wouldn't think of Ken and Debbie as my family. They don't like me. They don't think I'm a good mother, and they never thought I was good enough for Matt."

"That's a laugh."

"Emily!"

"It's true," Emily said.

"Maybe, but it's not nice."

"They aren't nice to you."

She ignored Emily this time, talking almost to herself. "The only thing we shared was Matt. We have no common ground to help us get along now, not even the kids." Becca stopped.

"Except—" Emily filled in "—your opposition to Jared's racing school."

"I haven't said I flat out oppose it. I have questions."

"You didn't get your answers when Jared met with you and Drew and Eli?"

"I got answers. I didn't like some of them. I'm trying to keep an open mind."

Her phone dinged another text message from Ken. The third one this evening. She pressed her lips together. *And I'm trying not to throw my support behind Jared simply because Ken's pressuring me to vote against it.*

"I want to know what other people think," Becca said. "That's what tonight's public hearing is about, giving everyone a chance to voice their views to help the other board members and me make the right decision."

"Sometimes the right thing is what *you* know is right for you, not what everyone else thinks is right."

"I can't say my track record is so great in the what's-right-for-me division."

"Becca." Exasperation laced Emily's voice. "You're not the first woman who married the wrong man."

Emily's words stung. Her friend didn't understand. She always tried, prayed to do the right thing, to make things right. And she usually succeeded, except for her marriage.

"Sorry for that," Emily said. "But are you sure you're just being open-minded and not using Jared's proposal as a way to distance yourself from him? Maybe because you're attracted to him?"

"Absolutely, not." What was with Emily that she kept pushing her at Jared? "I—"

"No, let me finish. Drew and Eli both work with kids, some of whom are in danger of getting offtrack—no pun intended. The kind of kids Jared wants to help. They don't agree with everything Jared has in his proposal, but they're behind the project. Drew told me you questioned the program starting with kids younger than middle school. You could support the project without letting Brendon participate if you think he's too young."

Easy enough for Emily to say. She wasn't the single parent who would have to tell Brendon that, no, he couldn't learn to race dirt bikes from his idol, Jared. Becca flopped back on the bed. She was so tired of everything being a struggle. What had she been thinking when she'd agreed to serve on the Zoning Board?

"Mommy," Emily's daughter called in the background. "Ryan hid my new Magic Markers Mrs. Cook gave me on the last day of school."

"I'd better go referee. Did you want a ride tonight?"

"No, I'd better drive myself. The board may want to stay after the hearing to discuss what people have said."

"Okay. Think about what I said. About Jared. And the racing school."

The beep of another text from the Sheriff muffled Emily's goodbye.

As if she could stop thinking about either Jared *or* his racetrack.

* * *

Jared and his attorney pulled up to the Schroon Town Hall forty-five minutes before the public hearing was scheduled to begin. A New York State Police cruiser sat off to the side of a line of sign-carrying protesters marching single file across the front of the building. The town had brought in the big guns.

"Nice welcoming committee," his attorney, Dan, said. "Looks like the same group I caught on the news the other night."

"The Albany station played it, too?"

"I think one of the regional news syndicates picked it up. You're news, man."

"Right. I've been news before. But usually good news." He'd enjoyed the limelight the first few years after he'd started winning races. Then, it had gotten old fast. Now, he was having second thoughts about having given up his publicist when he'd retired from motocross. Or maybe he should have connected with Emily when he first arrived. Anything he did now would seem like a reaction rather than action.

"You're still good news," Dan assured him before he dismissed the protesters. "What's twenty or thirty people?"

"More of the local population than you can imagine." Jared scanned the parking lot behind them. Several more cars had pulled in while they were talking. He watched a man about his age or a little older pull open the sliding passenger side door of a minivan. More protest signs? He stilled when the man pulled out a ramp and a woman in a wheelchair powered down it. Liz Whittan, the girl—woman—his father had injured driving drunk the fall of Jared's freshman year in high school. Her appearance would dredge up bad memories about Dad and him among the people at the hearing. Why was he even trying?

"We should go in," Dan said, his gaze following Jared's to Liz making her way across the parking lot.

Liz lifted her hand in a wave. "Jared. Jared Donnelly?"

"Someone you know?" Dan asked.

"Know of." Liz had been three or four grades ahead of him at school. "Old family business. Go on in."

Liz closed the distance between her van and Jared.

"As your attorney, I'll stay."

"Whatever." Maybe Dan was right to stay. He'd put his foot in his mouth in public before. His mind traveled back to his behavior in the months following his mentor's death. More times than he cared to remember.

"Jared, I thought it was you." Liz looked up at him and his stomach knotted.

Had his opponents stooped this low, or was Liz a ready participant?

"Liz Whittan," she said.

"I know who you are." He fought to keep his voice modulated.

She smiled, and he braced himself for what he expected she would say.

"I saw you when we drove in. This is my husband, Mike." She nodded at the man who had helped her out of the van. "I wanted to catch you before the hearing to tell you what a great idea I think your proposed project is."

"You like it?" The invisible bands cutting off air to his lungs snapped.

"Yes. I teach with Eli and Becca, middle school math, and have already made a mental list of some students I'd encourage to participate. You have a lot of people behind you."

Jared glanced at the protesters.

She waved them off. "Half of those people would be against their own mothers if they proposed anything new or different for the town. You have the support of people who could help you get your project off the ground."

His attorney smiled as if he'd had a part in this. Or maybe it was just relief that he wasn't representing a losing cause.

Liz ticked off the people on his side. "Anne Hazard and GreenSpaces, all of the Hazards, I think, the town supervisor, Harry Stowe, almost every teacher I've talked to, my pastor, the local business association and the Zoning Board, including Becca Norton."

"I'm not counting on Becca, not from what she's said to me." It hurt to say it out loud.

Liz gave him a knowing smile. "I've known Becca for a long time, since she started teaching at Schroon Lake. Trust me. She likes the idea. She just doesn't know it yet."

Jared wished he *could* trust her words.

Dan checked his watch. "We need to go in."

Jared moved to the side to let Liz and her husband go ahead. The protesters divided to let them through and closed ranks as Jared and his attorney followed.

"Take your racetrack somewhere else," the man closest to the door said.

"And yourself," came a woman's voice to Jared's left.

The state police officer stepped out of his car. Jared tensed as the line separated to let him and Dan into the Town Hall. The uplift he'd gotten from Liz's encouragement had dissipated like smoke in the wind when the officer had opened the car door. While he appreciated the officer's help, he was used to fighting his own battles, winning on his own merit.

Just inside the door, a sheriff's deputy Jared didn't

recognize stopped them. He pointed at the cardboard tube with the racing school plans Jared had in his hand.

"Sir, I'll need to see what's in that tube. No signage is allowed in the meeting."

"This is Jared Donnelly," Dan said.

"I'll handle this," Jared said, opening the tube and spreading out the sheets for the deputy to examine. He didn't need Dan stepping in for him any more than he'd needed the state police officer or anyone else.

A commotion from outside snapped Becca's and the other board members' attention to the doorway of the meeting room. Jared and his attorney entered and walked to the seats reserved for them in the front of the room. His mouth was set in a grim line that accented the planes of his face. He caught her staring and she looked past him to the room at large. With more than a half hour until the public hearing was scheduled to begin, it was already almost filled to capacity. She scanned the faces and saw many she recognized and a surprising number she didn't. For better or worse, Jared and his project had certainly activated the residents of Paradox Lake and the rest of the Town of Schroon.

She returned her gaze to Jared. He met it with a cool stare as he and his attorney walked past their seats to the dais. Her memory of Jared's expression when she'd said they needed to keep their distance and of his preferring to wait for Connor outside zipped down her spine in a virtual shudder. She'd watched from her window as he'd strode up the road out of sight. Even though she'd tossed and turned that night, every stray noise waking her up to thoughts about Jared, she still believed keeping her distance was the right decision.

"I have updated plans for you." His voice cut through

the buzz of the filled room. "They weren't ready until this afternoon. We were waiting for input from the Department of Transportation about the changes to the Route 9 access the GreenSpaces engineers are suggesting." He unrolled a set of plans from the cardboard tube.

"Good," Tom Hill said. "I've had a lot of questions about traffic on Route 9 and the possibility of a roundabout."

Jared's expression hardened. "And you won't find DOT's answers here. They didn't get back to Green-Spaces. These plans show the access with and without a roundabout."

"That's too bad," Tom said. "I know the people out that way are concerned about crowds and traffic, particularly on race days."

Tom glanced at her and back to Jared. "But I'm sure you know that."

Jared frowned and Becca's cheeks heated. What was that supposed to mean? Tom or his wife, Karen, must have heard Charlotte talking about her and Jared having dinner together on Saturday. Her heart thudded. To clear up any questions about her having a conflict of interest, she should have talked with Tom about Jared fixing her car and dinner before tonight's meeting. Who was she trying to kid? She had a conflict of interest all right, but it had nothing to do with Jared's racetrack and the Zoning Board. On that, she was confident she could be impartial. Her conflict of interest was between what her heart seemed to want and what she knew was best for her and her children.

"We'd better take a look at these before the meeting starts, although I'm sure you and your attorney will be able to provide up-to-date answers to any traffic questions we can't answer." Tom motioned Becca and the other board members to join him in a small side room.

As she followed, Becca overheard Jared's attorney ask, "Something you need to fill me in on? The board chair was talking about something other than the racing school."

"No. No, nothing at all."

She recoiled at the vehemence behind his words.

"Mr. Hill?" The sheriff's deputy poked his head in the side room a few minutes later. "We've reached room capacity, so I've closed the outside door and will monitor it. Here's the list of people who want to speak."

"Thanks." Tom took the clipboard and handed it to the board secretary. "We might as well get started." He rolled up the plans and led them back out to the larger room.

Despite several strategically placed fans, the packed room felt at least ten degrees hotter to Becca than the smaller one they'd come from.

Tom went through the formalities of opening the hearing. "Everyone who wants to speak should have a number. If you don't, see the deputy in the lobby."

A couple of people stood and walked to the lobby.

"All right. Whoever has number one, please come up to the microphone. You can address your questions to the board or to Mr. Donnelly and his attorney."

A man Becca didn't recognize walked to the mic.

"Please state your name and question," Tom said.

The man said his name. "Before I start, it's good to see that we have someone on the board who's on our side. From what I'd heard, I thought this mockery of decent living was a done deal."

Several whistles and cheers followed.

"Get to your question," Tom said.

"I just wanted to thank Mrs. Norton."

Becca caught Jared's narrow-eyed glare before she spoke. "Excuse me?"

"You're the one who set up the protest Saturday afternoon in front of the school, aren't you? I saw you handing out signs. Ken told me you were in our camp, your property being so close to Donnelly's—" he sneered his name "—and all."

A mental haze blocked everything but her view of Jared. His eyes blazed. He couldn't seriously think that she could have organized an afternoon protest in Schroon Lake and gone home and made dinner for him, even without considering that she hadn't had a car.

"Hey," someone else shouted from the back. "Shouldn't she excuse herself from the board decision? You're supposed to be neutral and vote on the merits of the project."

Tom's gavel came down with a bang. "I don't often get to do that," he said, lifting some of the tension in the room, although not in Jared from the rigid way he held himself.

"Becca?" Tom gave her the floor.

She stood on shaky knees, hoping no one noticed. Could her ex-father-in-law have set her up by getting someone who looked enough like her to organize the rally? But people who knew her would have had to know it wasn't her. "I had nothing to do with the rally on Saturday. I was home all afternoon and evening."

"Can you prove it?" someone else shouted.

Jared's supporters were as bad as the opposing guy who'd started all of this. She blinked. What was she doing, setting up an us-against-them scenario?

"I…"

Jared stood. She couldn't tell from his stony expression if he was going to defend her or join in the attack. His attorney touched his arm at the same time Tom brought his gavel down again.

"I know Mrs. Norton was home Saturday dinnertime," Jared said.

Tom gave her and Jared the same look he had earlier.

"And I talked to her on her home phone about two o'clock," Anne Hazard stood and said.

Becca had forgotten that Anne had called Saturday afternoon to let her know Ari had left her swimsuit and towel at their house and ask if Becca wanted her to bring it to church on Sunday. As Becca sat, she sneaked a look at Jared to see if Anne's words had had any effect on him. He was listening to something his attorney was saying. She didn't need to prove anything to him. So why did she feel as if she did?

"If we're done with this nonsense," Tom's voice boomed across the room, "I'd like to get this *informational* hearing going. Your question or *relevant* comment, sir."

The man made a comment about how the project would ruin the quality of life in the Paradox Lake area and detrimentally impact the tourist trade.

Over the next two hours, Becca's gaze kept returning to Jared trying to gauge his reaction to the questions and comments, which seemed to be balanced pro and con. The only time he veered from answering questions directed to him with straight, to-the-point facts was when someone asked about the racing program or the kids it would be designed for. Then, his passion brought the whole room alive.

As the minutes ticked toward eleven, Becca noticed Jared's attorney leave the room, come back, say something to Jared and, at Jared's curt nod, leave again.

Another person finished speaking and, instead of

calling the next number, Tom said, "It's getting late. I'm going to adjourn the hearing and continue it until next month."

A groan rippled across the room, punctuated by several shouts.

Tom glared the group into a dull hum. "Anne, you should have the DOT report by then?"

"DOT says no more than three weeks."

"A month should allow for any additional delay. We want everyone to have an opportunity to speak his or her opinion. If you have a number and haven't had a turn tonight, come up after we adjourn and see the board secretary before you leave to stay on the list. Deputy," Tom called out so the man could hear him in the hall. "Once the room has cleared, please allow anyone waiting outside for a chance to speak to come in and sign up with the secretary."

The deputy stepped into the doorway. "Will do."

"Then, can I have a motion from the board to end the meeting?"

Becca had her hand in the air before Tom had finished the sentence. The short-sleeved natural linen suit she'd worn turned out to be much too warm for the now-stifling room. She rubbed the base of her neck. Despite the two bottles of water she'd downed over the past three hours, she felt the start of a heat headache.

Another board member seconded the motion. Tom adjourned the hearing and walked past the departing board members to Becca. "Can you stay a couple minutes to talk, or do you need to pick the kids up?"

"The kids are with Matt in Connecticut." Her words came out more sharply than they should have. Tom certainly had nothing to do with Ken and Debbie keeping them there longer than the weekend.

Tom nodded. "Jared." He caught him as he rose and motioned him to the dais.

Jared, on the other hand, had everything to do with Matt's and Ken and Debbie's actions, even if it wasn't intentional.

"Come back to the side office where the fan does something for this heat so we can talk."

Becca and Jared filed in behind Tom, reminding Becca of her high school principal and the one time in her school career she'd been called to the office— for defacing school property. Her freshman year, she'd joined in a non-school-sanctioned egg "war" between the cheerleaders and the football players on school property the evening before the big homecoming game. Afterwards, she and another cheerleader had written "Go Wildcats" on the cafeteria windows with soap crayon. A teacher who'd driven by had reported her and the others she'd recognized to the principal.

She glanced over her shoulder at Jared. His mouth was drawn in the grim line she was beginning to think was his natural expression. Or was he having the same déjà vu? For all Jared's high school bad-boy cred, she didn't remember him being a standard feature in the principal's office as some of the other guys had been.

"Sit." Tom waited until they'd taken seats on the opposite sides of the small rectangular table before he sat at the head of the table. He looked from Becca to Jared. "What is going on with you two?"

"Ladies first," Jared said. He didn't know if Becca had said anything to Tom about him fixing her car. About the rest, Tom probably had a good idea, given what he'd said at the hearing when Becca had been accused of being behind the protest on Saturday. Or as good an idea as anyone, since Jared wasn't sure himself what was or wasn't going on between he and Becca. When the guy at the hearing had pressed to have Becca excuse herself from the board vote, Jared had almost believed she'd organized the protest, was working with her ex-in-laws—despite what she'd said to him Saturday night. It wouldn't have been the first time he'd been duped by a woman or believed someone he'd cared about when he knew he shouldn't. It had taken him years to wise up to his father.

He looked across the table at her delicate profile illuminated by the track lighting overhead and remembered the softness of her skin when he'd brushed her jaw while fastening his motorcycle helmet on her. *No.* He hadn't believed it. He wanted to believe it to help build the wall between them that she wanted, and he needed, to maintain his focus on his project and his mission.

"Nothing, really," Becca said.

Despite the truthfulness of her words, they stung his masculine pride.

"Come on," Tom said. "Before the next hearing, I need to know if I should ask you to excuse yourself from debating and voting on Jared's project."

He looked at Jared as if he would, could, step in and clear things up for him.

Becca twisted the mother's ring with Brendon's and Ari's birthstones that she wore on her right hand. "My car wouldn't start after work last Friday. It was the alternator. Jared was driving by and stopped. I'd tried to call you but couldn't get through. Jared said you and Karen were on vacation."

Tom nodded and she rushed on. "He said he'd take a look at it and fix it if he could. We made a deal that I'd buy the parts and pay him for his labor with a home-cooked meal." She stopped.

"That's it?" Tom scratched his head.

"He did a few other things. To the car."

Jared stepped in man-to-man. "You know how it is. I finished the alternator and started looking at other things." He grinned at Tom.

Tom grinned back. "Yeah, I know how that goes. Then, you're not dating or whatever you kids call it now?"

"No," Becca said quickly. "Absolutely not."

She might as well have added *never*.

"And I'll be paying Jared the going rate for the other work. I've looked everything up online."

He wanted to say she could take as long as she needed, but not in front of Tom.

"Good," Tom said. "I don't see any conflict of interest at this point."

"I'll recuse myself before the vote if I see any problem," Becca said.

"Sounds good. You two go on home. I've got to lock up."

Jared pushed away from the table and stopped. About a half hour before the public hearing had adjourned, he'd told Dan he could leave since it was getting so late and Dan had a long drive back to Albany. Jared had figured he could catch a ride with one of the Hazards. They all lived just up the road from the parsonage. Except they were long gone.

"Uh." He cleared his throat. "I need a lift home. I came with Dan and he had to leave."

"I—" Becca started.

"No problem." Tom talked over her. "I go right by the parsonage."

"Thanks," Jared said.

Becca snapped her mouth shut, and Jared realized he'd spoken too soon. Unless his guess was wrong—and he didn't think it was—she'd been about to offer him a ride. He shouldn't have been so quick to accept Tom's offer. Jared shook off his disappointment. *No.* It was better for both of them if he took her direction from the other night and kept his distance.

Chapter Nine

Jared padded downstairs in his cutoff jeans, Autodromo Daniel Bonara racetrack muscle shirt and bare feet. After tossing and turning for hours, he'd finally fallen asleep in the early hours of the morning and had slept almost to eleven. With the public hearing continued to next month, he had a lot of time on his hands. Maybe he'd grab a breakfast sandwich at the General Store and wash his bike this morning, then call Emily about getting together to talk about promotion. It couldn't hurt to get his information out there over the next few weeks.

The parsonage phone rang. He waited a moment for his brother to pick up the other extension in his home office, then slipped on his shoes and started for the front door.

"Jared." Connor's shout stopped him. "The phone's for you. I'll bring it down."

He couldn't just pick up the extension down here?

Connor bounded down the stairs, handed him the phone and waited.

"Hello."

"Hello," the woman at the other end said. "I'm looking for Jared M. Donnelly." The woman stumbled in her speech. "Pastor Donnelly said you're Jared M. Donnelly."

He frowned at his brother. Somehow a fan—or worse, some race bunny—had gotten their home phone number.

"Jared M. Donnelly, who used to live at…" The woman gave the address of the house on Daniels Road where he and his brothers had grown up.

The way the woman kept using his middle initial was odd. He hadn't used it professionally. One more way to separate him from his namesake. "Yes," he answered without thinking.

"Finally."

Jared could hear relief in the woman's voice.

"My name is Chris Sutton. We live in Morrisonville, outside of Plattsburgh. I have your daughter, Hope."

Not again! Jared clenched the phone. He'd been through one false paternity suit following his wild time after his mentor's death. It was not something he wanted to go through again.

"I don't think so."

"But…" Her voice wavered. "You said you were Jared M. Donnelly. That you'd lived on Daniels Road. Your name is on Hope's birth certificate." Her voice grew stronger with a tinge of desperation, "I suppose you're going to tell me there's another Jared Donnelly in Paradox Lake."

"This conversation is over." He hung up.

"What was that?"

"Some woman trying to claim I'm the father of her child. Says my name is on the girl's birth certificate as her father."

"Could you be?"

Jared glared his answer. *Not likely in Plattsburgh, at least.* He pushed the possibility of elsewhere to the back of his mind. It wasn't that he didn't like kids. With his racing school, he was planning to devote his career to helping kids. And he'd certainly take financial responsibility if he had a child. But he wasn't father material. He had no frame of reference.

"I know that New York State requires a father to sign an acknowledgment of paternity before he can be listed on the birth certificate."

Jared ignored his brother's raised eyebrow at his knowing that information. "I didn't sign any acknowledgment. And the woman had the audacity to get sarcastic and say she supposed I was going to tell her there was another Jared Donnelly in Paradox Lake."

Jared and Connor stared at each other. "Dad," they said in unison.

Jared punched the callback button on the phone. "Ms. Sutton?" he said to the woman who answered. "This is Jared Donnelly. Sorry I hung up on you. I think it's my father, not me, you're looking for."

"Hope's father *was* ten or so years older than her mother." The woman's relief at his callback was obvious. "Can you put me in touch with him?"

"No, I'm sorry. We haven't seen or heard from him in almost seven years. How old is Hope?"

"Six."

That fit with his father's disappearance. He would have been in his late forties when she'd been born.

"You're not the girl's mother?" he asked.

"No, I'm her day-care provider. Her mother died four years ago, but Hope always lived with her grandmother. After your father, you'd be Hope's closest living relative."

Why was this woman looking for his father now if her mother had died four years ago? Something didn't sound right.

Chris Sutton continued, "Her grandmother passed a couple of weeks ago. She had a heart attack but seemed to be doing well until she picked up an infection in the hospital. She was only fifty-nine. When she was seemingly recovering, Hope's grandmother had me go to her house, get her strongbox and bring it to the hospital. She gave me Hope's birth certificate and the Acknowledgment of Paternity your father signed. She said if anything happened to her, Hope had family on her father's side in Paradox Lake."

"And that would be us." Jared felt as drained as if he had just finished a round of weight training at the gym.

"When can you come? I've been telling Hope that we would find her daddy. I probably shouldn't have kept her after the funeral, but she was so lost and is used to us. I hated the thought of contacting Child Protective Services. My husband spent five years in the foster care system until he was adopted when he was ten. We didn't want that for Hope if she had family."

"I want to talk with my dad's stepmother, and an attorney."

"I understand." The woman sounded skeptical, as if he'd blow her off.

"I'll let you know as soon as possible." The Donnellys, except for his father, took care of their own. That was one of the reasons he'd returned. He hung up and turned to Connor. "Apparently, we have a little sister."

Jared filled Connor in on the details and pulled his cell phone from his pocket to call his attorney. He pressed "contacts" and stopped. "Connor," he called to his brother, who was heading back to his office. "Do you have a business card from the lawyer who handled Bert Miller's estate?"

"Yeah. It's in the drawer of the coffee table."

Jared shuffled through the drawer and pulled out the card. It would be better to use a separate lawyer for this private matter rather than his business attorney. Although he didn't know Bert's lawyer beyond the time he and his brothers had spent with him at the reading of Bert's will, his card said family law, and Jared was willing to trust Bert's judgment.

He made his calls and was surprised at how quickly he was able to pull things together. And he didn't care that he'd played his celebrity card with the law office to do it.

Eight hours later, he pulled into the parsonage garage with Hope fast asleep in a booster seat in the back of his car, a hole torn in his heart by the rage he felt for his father's actions and Hope's quiet sobs that hadn't stopped until she'd fallen asleep about halfway home. The attorney had said he would take care of all the custody details, that there shouldn't be any problem making Jared Hope's guardian since his—and Hope's—father had been missing for years.

He got out, opened the back door and gazed at his little sister. As Gram had said, even if the Suttons hadn't had Hope's documents, there would have been little question that she was a Donnelly. Except for the length of her hair, she looked exactly like Jared had in his kindergarten school photo.

"Time to wake up, Hope," he coaxed as he unfastened the straps to her booster seat. Gram had said it would be better to wake her up so she could see the house and where she was sleeping before they tucked her in for the night.

Her eyes opened wide and she let out a scream. "I want my Grammy. I want Chris."

He hugged her to him and carried her into the house, silently praying, *Dear Lord, I know You don't give us more than we can handle, but this has to be close. Please guide me to do what's best for Hope because I have no idea what to do with a six-year-old little girl, let alone one who has lost everyone close to her.*

"You'd think he'd have the decency to bring her somewhere other than the church parsonage," Debbie Norton said.

"Hmm?" Becca sat at her desk in the small day-care office reviewing the list of kids preregistered for Vacation Bible School next week. The Sheriff had dropped off Debbie and the kids about fifteen minutes earlier. He'd needed to run to the General Store for fishing bait and thought she and Debbie could catch up while he did. So far, the catching up had been about how much the kids had wanted to stay at their father's, but Matt and Crystal were entertaining this weekend, so Crystal had needed to get the house ready.

As usual, business and socializing came first with Matt.

Becca had work she needed to finish today, so she half listened while Debbie prattled on.

"Jared Donnelly," Debbie said.

Becca gave Debbie her full attention.

"He has a daughter, you know. It has to be his daughter. One of my friends texted me. She saw them at the soft-serve ice-cream stand. Said the little girl looked exactly like him." Debbie paused for effect. "Seriously, what kind of father could that man be? The things Ken read about him in those racing and celebrity magazines. Disgusting."

Becca's grip on her pen tightened. Debbie's mention of Jared's offtrack life while he'd been on the circuit brought up her inner questions about how well she knew him. The fact was she had trouble picturing his reported wildness. But that could be because she didn't want to. If Debbie was right, he had an illegitimate daughter, a fact he hadn't thought to mention to her or, evidently, anyone else. Becca placed the pen on her desk and flexed her fingers. The little girl must live with her mother, and if she spent time with Jared, he must still have some kind of relationship with the mother, even if it was just as parents.

Becca pushed those thoughts to the back of her mind. "*If* Jared has a daughter, where else would she stay? Jared lives at the parsonage."

"About that, I've heard talk that some of the Community Church parishioners want to ask Pastor Connor to tell his brother to live elsewhere. The vote to call Pastor was close, and I suspect some people regret their vote now."

Becca didn't have to think hard to guess how her ex-in-laws had voted.

"I assume you're taking Ken's advice and staying clear of Jared."

Becca pushed the list she'd been checking to the side. Debbie must not have heard about Jared and her Saturday night dinner. If she or the Sheriff confronted her about it, Becca could honestly say that she'd cut whatever fragile ties might have been developing between them. It disgusted her that Matt and his parents always had her walking on eggshells. But the alternative of a custody battle seemed worse.

"The girl is about Ari's age. You wouldn't want Ari to become friendly with *her*. It's enough that Brendon has a misplaced infatuation with that man."

Becca slapped her hand on the desk and her ex-mother-in-law started. "Debbie, you're talking about a little girl. If she's going to be staying, visiting for any length of time, making friends here may make her more comfortable. I'll mention to Pastor Connor that Jared might want to enroll her in Vacation Bible School."

"Well." Debbie huffed. "I suppose that might help her. Her father is certainly no role model."

Actually, a lot of people Becca had talked with thought he was, despite the stories about him that had appeared in the entertainment magazines. She wasn't going to argue that point with Debbie now. She just wanted Ken to come pick up Debbie so she could get back to her work.

"Ready?" the Sheriff said from the doorway.

"Yes, we're all caught up," his wife said.

"Good." He fixed his gaze on Becca. "And nice job at the Zoning Board meeting. Putting up a facade of neutrality was good. Keep people guessing while you work to stop that no-good interloper Donnelly."

Becca got up and closed the office door after looking in the hall to make sure no children had heard the Sheriff badmouthing Jared. Holding the doorknob, she said, "Tell me. Did you orchestrate the protest in Schroon Lake on Saturday?"

"Sure did." An oily smile spread across his face. "Pretty clever of me to hire that woman who looked like you, if I do say so myself."

"Clever isn't the word that comes to my mind."

His smile widened. "Did Debbie tell you about Matt taking the kids to Florida later this summer?"

Her chest tightened. "No."

"A business trip with the kids and Crystal coming along. Matt's up for a big promotion to the main office there. If all goes well, we may all be moving down there by the end of the summer."

Becca's heart stopped. She knew Matt couldn't move the kids to Florida without her consent, even if he had custody, which he was unlikely to be able to arrange by the end of the summer. Even if the Sheriff owned the Family Court judge, which he didn't. But the threat was clear.

"So you two have definitely decided to retire to Florida, then?"

"Like I said, we may *all* be moving to Florida. Come on, Deb."

Becca resisted heaving the coffee mug on the desk at the back of the Sheriff's head as he and Debbie opened the office door and walked out. She was still shaking a couple of minutes later when Brendon darted in.

"Hi, Mom. Can I talk with you? Ms. Leanne said it was okay to come in from the playground."

"Sure." The work she had could wait. "Did you have a good time at your dad's?"

"It was okay. The picnic thing, at least. The rest of the time, Dad was either working at home or at his office, and Crystal kept telling us to go watch TV or play in our rooms and followed us around like she was afraid we'd steal or break something." He scuffed the toe of his sneaker against the vinyl floor. "I don't think she likes us."

"Sure she does. She's just not used to having kids around." Becca suspected that Crystal wasn't fond of any kids, not that she particularly disliked Brendon and Ari.

"If she doesn't like kids around and Dad works all of the time, why did he say we'll be spending a lot more time at his house? Do I have to?"

Brendon's words took her back again to her begging her father to not make her go to stay at her mother's. *No, not if I have any say in it, and I do.*

"I'll talk with your father. I'm sure we'll work it out."

"Thanks, Mom. You're the greatest. See you later."

She tried to go back to her work. If only she had half the confidence in handling her life as Brendon did.

Becca put her paperwork away. Since she wasn't getting anything done anyway, she might as well head to the Fellowship Hall to be on hand to greet parents picking up their children. They tended to come earlier on Fridays.

"Hey." Jared's baritone pulled her from her jumble of thoughts about her ex-in-laws, Matt and the kids.

"Hi. Looking for your brother? He should still be in his office unless the toddler teacher has him reading the 'twos' a story. He made a lot of little friends the day he subbed in that class."

"No, I'm looking for you."

Her heart raced. "What can I do for you?"

"I need to explain, run something by you. It was Connor's idea actually."

"It's not about your racetrack? I'm taking Tom's advice and avoiding any appearance of conflict of interest." *Especially after the Sheriff's setup on Saturday and today's attempt at coercion.*

"It's not about the racing school. But it's as important. More important."

Something in his voice, even more than his words, made her really look at him. She saw lines around his mouth she hadn't noticed before and fatigue in his eyes.

"Do you want to come in the school office?"

"Yes."

"Pull up a chair." Becca sat behind the desk before it struck her that it might have been better for him to have left the chair by the wall and her to have taken the adjacent seat. It was the teacher in her. She was used to having a desk buffer.

He sat in the chair, his presence seeming to take up

more space than the Sheriff and Debbie combined. "Connor thinks I should volunteer to help with Vacation Bible School next week."

When Debbie had been maligning the little girl, and Becca had said she'd suggest to Connor that Jared enroll his daughter in VBS, she hadn't thought about Jared being part of the package. She pasted a smile on her face. "We're always looking for more volunteers."

"No." He shot out of his seat and stalked back and forth in front of the desk. "It's not really about VBS. It's Hope, our sister."

The little girl was Jared's illegitimate sister, not his daughter. It shouldn't make a difference. Everyone made mistakes, and the Lord forgave them all. But, as much as her thought bothered her, it did make a difference. She waited for him to go on.

He dropped back into the chair. "Connor and I found out Wednesday that we have a six-year-old sister named Hope." He explained the sad circumstances, how he and his grandmother had brought her back to Paradox Lake and he'd taken custody of her as her closest and oldest living relative. "She's hardly done anything the past two days except cry and ask to go home. But she doesn't have any home but ours now."

He slumped as if his feeling of helplessness was more than he could handle.

"The poor little thing." Becca reached across the desk and touched his hand. He recoiled as if stung before reaching back and covering her hand with his. She squeezed his thumb hoping to give back some of the strength he'd given her when he'd held her Saturday night.

He gave her a halfhearted smile. "I know there isn't the stigma against illegitimate children there once was. But poor little Hope is Jerry Donnelly's daughter, a daughter young enough to be his granddaughter. My parents were still married when she was born. Some people are going to talk." His expression hardened. "While I don't care what people say about me—" Becca wasn't as sure about that as he seemed to be "—I care about what people might say about Hope."

"And you're looking for your church family to help. I'll call Autumn Hazard-Hanlon tonight and put Hope on the church prayer chain, if Connor hasn't already."

"Thanks. Eli put me in touch with the counselor for the lower grades at the Schroon Lake school." He seemed to be searching for words.

"Yes, I know her. She's great with the kids."

He breathed in and out. "She's going to work with Hope. But she suggested being with other kids might help. Connor came up with the VBS idea. Gram is going to be here, too."

Becca nodded. Mrs. Stowe had been helping with VBS for as long as she remembered.

"I'd like to register Hope."

"Sure thing." Becca pulled out the registration list she'd been going over earlier to make class assignments.

"What grade will Hope be going into in the fall?"

"I have no idea. I have a bunch of papers. But I've been up almost thirty hours straight. I haven't looked at them."

Becca sympathized. It had to be almost like having a new infant. She remembered well being up all night with Ari and having no one to relieve her. "No problem. I'll put Hope in the class with the kids who have finished kindergarten or first grade. Your grandmother is helping Karen with that class, and Ari will be in it."

"Good. Maybe they'll be friends."

"I'll talk with Ari."

"Thanks. I'll see you Monday. No, Sunday. We'll be at church. Gram is doing the children's program."

"Right. I'll put you to work Monday with the fifth and sixth graders. We seem to have a decided majority of boys this year."

As she listened to Jared walk down the hall, against her better judgment, all she could think of was how his volunteering would allow them to be together without his project or her ex-in-laws between them. How pathetic was that?

"Jared, can you sit with my class when we get ice cream?"

He looked into wide blue eyes that mirrored his own and his insides melted faster than the July sun would melt the soft-serve ice cream VBS was providing as an after-closing treat.

"Sure, Hope. I'll have the kids from my class sit near us and let Ms. Leanne know what we're doing so she can help me keep an eye on them."

Hope favored him with one of her rare, but more frequent, smiles.

"Should we ask Connor to sit with us?" he asked.

"I guess. He's my brother, too."

Jared warmed at Hope's preference for him.

"But you *have* to ask Ms. Becca. She's Ari's mother, you know. And I like her."

He did, too. More than was good for him. "I know. But won't Ari ask her to sit with your class?"

He and Becca had gotten along well working with the kids this week, but she'd kept a professional distance.

"Yeah, but you're bigger and a man. My grammy, not your grandma, said that my mommy would do anything a man asked her to do."

Sadness settled over him. "Ms. Becca seems to do what she wants to do, not what other people tell her. And what God tells her is right."

"Like we learned in our Bible story yesterday," Hope said.

"Just like that." He stopped himself from giving her the hug he wanted to. He and Connor had learned that Hope wasn't ready for the hugs and kisses and tickles that had been a part of their childhood with their mother and grandparents.

"Okay, everyone." Connor pitched his voice above the din of the children and adults milling around the church hall. "Line up with your class. If a parent or other special visitor is driving you to the soft-serve stand, he or she can pick you up from your class. If not, stay with your teacher. Either Jared or Mrs. Hill will be driving you in the church van or her minivan."

Hope tugged at the hem of his T-shirt. "Does that mean I can ride with you because you're my special visitor?"

"It certainly does."

"Ari and her mommy, too?"

"No, I think they'll be driving their own car."

"Oh. But we can still sit with them, right?"

"Right. We should be able to sit with them." From growing up with his father, he knew better than to make promises he might not be able to keep.

Fifteen minutes later, Jared and Becca were at the soft-serve stand's outside service window handing cones to the fifth and sixth graders. The younger children had been served first, and Karen Hill and his grandmother had taken Hope and Ari with the rest of their class to a large picnic table shaded by a tall stand of pines.

"That takes care of the kids," Jared said. "What's your pleasure?"

"Vanilla chocolate swirl," Becca said.

Jared ordered Becca's cone and a vanilla one for himself and pulled out his wallet.

"You don't have to pay for your cone," Becca said. "I have the money here." She patted her pocket. "From the VBS fund."

"I don't have to. I want to." He placed a one hundred dollar bill on the window counter.

Her eyes widened. "Not for the whole school."

"Why not? It's a contribution. For the kids. You'll have more money for next year."

"I guess."

"What if I say I cleared it with Connor?"

"In that case…"

"I didn't say I did. I said *what if.*"

She laughed and slugged him in the arm.

The server returned with their cones and he settled up.

"Are you calling me a liar?" Hope's high-pitched voice carried across the parking lot to them. He strode toward the table with Becca at his heels.

"Jared doesn't look like a brother," Ari argued back. "Brendon is a brother. Jared looks more like a daddy."

Jared held his breath, ready to referee if Hope burst into tears, her usual way of handing any tension and her grief. Not that he could blame her, not with all she'd been through.

"He is, too, my brother."

Becca brushed ahead of him as if to intervene. He grabbed her elbow. "Wait. Let them go for a second. This is the first I've seen her show any spirit. She hardly talks at home."

Becca's look of pity encompassed them both.

"Jared and me don't know where our daddy is. He's probably dead like my mommy and grammy."

He ignored the black look Becca gave him. Did she think he'd told Hope that? He rushed over, ready for the expected torrent of tears.

"I'll let Jared be your big brother, too, or Connor or Josh, if you want."

"Pastor Connor is your brother, too?" Ari asked in disbelief.

"Of course, silly. He and Josh are Jared's brothers, so they're mine, too."

"No fair," Ari said. "All I have is Brendon. And my daddy in Connecticut."

His throat went scratchy. Ari's last words sounded like an afterthought. He knew only too well what an absent father felt like, although his had been physically present.

"Jared and Connor and Josh are better than any old daddy." Hope stuck out her lower lip.

Jared's heart swelled at her words. Of course, they wouldn't have to be much to be better than her father.

"Isn't that sweet?" Becca whispered, placing her hand on his forearm and infusing him with an altogether different kind of warmth.

She pulled her hand away. "Watch it. Your ice cream."

He felt her gaze on him as he licked the drip off of his hand and the cone.

She cleared her throat. "If Hope feels comfortable with the kids, you might want to sign her up for a couple days or half days here. We have an opening in her age group."

"Connor and I talked about that."

"I'll text you over the weekend what you need to have to register her. That way, if you decide to, you can come in next week and do the paperwork."

"We'll see." He was torn. He needed some respite from

taking care of Hope so he could work on his racing-school project. But he wanted to reassure her that he was there for her, wasn't going to go away as everyone else in the little girl's life had.

"Mommy," Ari said. "We saved you and Jared a seat."

The girls scooted down the picnic table bench to make room for them. Becca slid in, then Jared.

"Can you hold my cone?" Becca asked handing it to him before he was able to answer.

She pulled several napkins out of the dispenser in the middle of the table, and he watched in admiration as she deftly mopped the ice cream off both Ari's and Hope's faces and hands.

"Thanks." She took her cone back and started eating it without missing a beat.

He listened to the girls' chatter and Becca's comments as they ate their ice cream. He wasn't sure if it was her teacher's training or a natural affinity for children, but Becca made parenting look far easier than he was finding it to be.

"Better round up the troops," Jared said when they'd finished. Before he rose to gather the kids who had ridden to the soft-serve stand in the church van with him, an older woman stopped at their table.

"What a beautiful family you have. I've been watching the girls. I couldn't help it. They're so cute. Are they twins? It's adorable how much the one looks like her mother and the other so much like you."

Jared and Becca stared at her. "Thank you," Becca choked out.

"I'm sorry," the woman said, introducing herself. "I'm here visiting my daughter and her family. They recently moved here and are looking for a home church, so they enrolled the kids in VBS. They've had a great week."

She laughed. "I know. More than you needed to know. My daughter tells me that all the time. You make such a nice family. I couldn't resist stopping and telling you so."

Jared opened his mouth, but no words came out. No one had ever referred to his family as a nice family.

"How kind of you to say that." Becca filled the gap in the conversation. "But we're not—"

"Sorry," the woman said. "My daughter is waving to me to leave."

Jared watched her scurry off. She'd probably find out soon enough that they weren't a family, nice or otherwise. He glanced sideways at Becca and the girls. But for a moment, he was going to let himself forget about all of the complications in his life and allow himself to pretend.

Chapter Ten

"Come on, guys, get a move on." Becca herded the kids out to the car. It was her week to open The Kids' Place at six-forty-five to be ready for parents who had to drop their kids off at seven. Brendon dragged himself out and into the backseat, a stark contrast to Ari, who bounced out and chatted away as Becca checked the buckle on her booster seat.

"You're awful quiet this morning," she said to her son. "Too early for you?"

"No."

Becca glanced at the rearview mirror. He was staring out the side window. She knew he'd rather not have to go to day care with her every day. None of his friends did. But it was only one summer. Next year, God willing, her finances would be better and she'd be able to stay home with Brendon and Ari as she had other summers. She bit her lip. Unless Matt sued her successfully for joint custody and her child support payments were reduced.

"Mom," Brendon said after she'd driven a couple of miles. "I think Dad wants us to come to his house next weekend."

"Did he call you last night?" She tried to keep her

voice nonchalant. Ever since Matt had given Brendon the cell phone, he and the Sheriff had been calling Brendon rather than her about arranging visits, in violation of their custody agreement. Usually, Brendon brought the phone right to her.

"He must have called after I fell asleep. He left a voice message. He sounds funny like before he left and he used to come home late and you guys would fight."

Becca gripped the steering wheel until her knuckles were white. Brendon had been a toddler then. Her heart sunk. She'd had no idea he'd heard or remembered.

"Here, listen. He says something about coming to get us or Grandpa coming to get us on Friday and something about Florida." Brendon played the message.

Matt was clearly drunk. As Brendon had said, Matt rambled on about coming to get the kids on Friday and, then, about the Sheriff and Debbie bringing Brendon and Ari to Connecticut on Friday. After that, he went off about Florida and his job and Disney World.

She swallowed the bile in her throat. "Does your father ever sound like that when you stay with him?"

"He did a little after the picnic he took us to."

Her shoulders tensed. "Did he drive you home after the picnic?"

"No, Grandpa drove us. Dad and Crystal rode in their 370z. It only has two seats."

"Promise me you won't get in the car with him or let Ari if you see that your father's been drinking beer or anything else with alcohol or if he sounds funny like that."

"We always ride with Grandpa and Grandma. She says it's too much of a pain to move Ari's booster seat." Brendon's voice dropped a couple decibels. "But I think she knows Dad drinks too much."

The pain she felt for Brendon overshadowed her tension. "Promise me, anyway."

"I promise. I'm not stupid. I've seen the TV commercials. So, do we have to go to Dad's or what? Grandpa says we have to go to Dad and Crystal's whenever they say. It's in some agreement you guys have."

Now wasn't the time to explain her and Matt's agreement, but if Matt was going to start using his visitation rights, the kids, Brendon especially, were old enough to know the basic details. And, as sad as it made her, she needed to sit Ari down and talk with her in six-year-old terms about not riding with Matt if he'd been drinking.

"I'll talk to your dad and Grandma or Grandpa."

"Tell them this weekend isn't good for me. Remember, it's Ian's birthday and they're having a campout party at the lake."

"I remember."

"I don't want to go, either," Ari said. "Crystal doesn't like us and Daddy smells funny like he has bad breath."

"I said I'd talk to your dad." Old memories and fears made her voice sharper than she mean it to be. "We'll work something out."

None of them said anything for the rest of the drive. She'd always honored their visitation agreement, which gave Matt the right to have the kids every other weekend. She'd generously given that right to the Nortons on many of the weekends in the past when Matt hadn't wanted them. She could honor the letter of the agreement, but she couldn't force the kids to *want* to spend time with their father. With the Sheriff pressuring her about her vote on Jared's racing school and his keeping tabs on her, now wasn't the time to tell Brendon and Ari they didn't have to go to their father's if they didn't want to. That would give Matt and the Nortons a legitimate reason to take her to Family Court, not that *she* didn't have one.

Talking to her ex-in-laws about Matt's drinking and her concern for the kids wasn't a real option, despite Debbie's possible realization that Matt had a problem. She'd tried before, and the Sheriff had dismissed her concerns, saying it was part of Matt's job to socialize. Becca wasn't at all sure Debbie would go against her husband, even for the kids. The one person she *would* talk with was her attorney to see if she had any recourse other than the one Becca wanted to spare the kids—Family Court.

She turned in to the church parking lot. It would help her if she could talk with someone who knew where she was coming from. Becca ran through her options. Her pastor was out. Although Connor had a firsthand understanding, he'd been one of her history students. It would be weird. The only other person she knew who would understand her fears and what the kids might be feeling was Jared. And she was trying her best not to let their relationship cross the line from casual friends to close personal friends.

Once the other day-care teachers began arriving, Becca left the parent greeting to them and went back to the office to try to catch Matt on the phone before he left for work.

"Hello," Crystal answered in a jovial tone.

"Hi. It's Becca. Is Matt there?"

"No." Crystal dropped the cheerfulness. "He's at the office."

For a moment, Becca considered bypassing Matt altogether and telling Crystal that the kids couldn't come this weekend, like he and the Sheriff tried to sidestep her by calling Brendon. *No, that would be sinking to their level.*

"Thanks, I'll call him there." She hung up and punched in the other phone number.

"Good morning, Matt Norton."

"Matt, we need to talk about the kids' visit next weekend. They won't be able to come. Brendon's best friend is having a birthday party campout on Saturday."

"Mom and Dad are bringing the kids again?"

He didn't even remember calling Brendon. Becca grit her teeth. "You left a drunken message on Brendon's phone that seemed to say that."

"Don't start," he warned.

"Or what? You'll take me to Family Court for full custody?" Becca let her anger get the best of her.

Matt backed off. "This weekend is bad for us, too. And Crystal's complaining that it seems like Mom and Dad are bringing them down here every weekend."

Every other weekend, as our custody agreement stipulates. "Good," she said. "I'll tell Brendon that he can go to the party. I've already talked with him about your drinking and not riding with you when you're drunk."

"You what?"

"I talked with him about your drinking, and I'm going to talk with Ari. I won't have you putting them in danger.

"Come on."

Becca cut him short. "We're done. Goodbye." She hung up before he could go into one of his tirades and closed her eyes until she'd stopped shaking.

"Hey." Jared's voice startled her. "I'm here to register Hope for day care. Karen said to come back and that she'd keep Hope with her class until I finished."

"Come in. I'm glad you and your brothers decided to sign her up."

He placed a manila folder on her desk and pulled a chair over. "We figure we can use all of the help we can

get. Gram has been great. Hope's used to having a grandmother mother figure. But I'm out of my element." He
dropped his gaze. "You know my dad wasn't much of a
father. Much of a man, really. I want to do what's right
for Hope."

Becca got up and closed the door for privacy. Any
teachers or kids passing by in the hall didn't need to hear
their conversation. She'd do the same for any parent en-
rolling his or her child.

"Thanks," he said as she sat back down.

She reassured him. "You probably know more about
parenting than you think. You used to take care of your
brothers for your mother."

He shrugged. "Yeah, Mom needed the help."

"And you gave it to her. They've both grown into decent Christian men."

"I'm not sure what part I had in that. I left home when
Josh was fourteen and Connor was eleven, and Dad was
getting worse. I wasn't there for them or Mom when they
needed me."

"You were eighteen, no older than the kids in my senior classes. You wanted to get on with your life."

His voice dropped. "That's why I came back. For
them, and to help other kids here like us, like Hope, and
parents like Mom who need support with their kids. The
only way I know to help is motocross racing. It's what I
know. It's what helped me."

Becca's heart filled with warmth that he was letting
her see inside him. She suspected it wasn't something he
did often or lightly.

He stopped. "Sorry."

"You don't have to be sorry for sharing with me."

"No, about bringing up my project after Tom's talk

with us the other night. I don't want to put you in a touchy position."

"Telling me what's behind your wanting to build your track here won't cause a conflict of interest. In fact, it may help me clarify things and, when the time comes, make the best decision for everyone."

"But that's not why I'm here. I'm here to register Hope." His crooked smile spoke his embarrassment at making Becca privy to his private feelings.

"Move your chair around next to me, and I'll go over your application and our basic rules and objectives here at the center."

Although her invitation had been no different than she would have given any parent registering a child, the office walls seemed to close in once Jared had moved his chair. Becca blocked out the faint scent of his woodsy aftershave and concentrated on reviewing the papers he'd brought and answering his questions.

"That should do it." She placed his application and the other documentation the center needed in a pile on her desk and closed his folder. "Any other questions?"

She looked up to see him staring at her intently.

"No, I'm good. Thanks. For everything. Your and the VBS volunteers' acceptance of Hope means so much to me—and Connor and Josh." He leaned toward her.

Her thoughts flitted to how he'd comforted her after dinner at her house, how she felt in his arms. She let his gaze draw her in and stilled as he lowered his head. So much for keeping her distance. He was going to kiss her. And against her better judgment, she was going to let him. She met his lips and he brushed them across hers. Calm rained over her, silencing the kernel of doubt that had started to say *good girls don't*.

A sharp rap on the office door jerked them apart.

"Becca." Leanne opened the door and glanced from her to Jared. "I didn't know you had someone with you."

"Jared's registering Hope for day care." *And pulling the foundation of my carefully controlled life out from under me.* "We just finished."

Leanne continued to look at Jared. Did she suspect something? No, that was silly. What could she suspect? Becca always closed the door for parent interviews.

"What's up?" she asked.

"We're short on juice for snack. I wanted to get the debit card to run up to the store for some."

Becca unlocked the top drawer of the desk, retrieved the card and handed it to Leanne.

"Thanks," Leanne said and left.

Jared lifted the folder from the desk. "One more thing."

Becca's heart constricted. He *wasn't* going to apologize for the kiss, say it was a mistake. She wouldn't let him. She could have stopped him. If she'd wanted to.

"I don't think I have Hope's booster seat fastened in my truck correctly. I was reading that seventy-five percent of kids' car seats are installed wrong or are the wrong size for the kid. I figured car seats would be something you'd know about."

A laugh of relief bubbled out. Leave it to a man to look up and quote statistics. "Car seats *are* something I know about. The beginning of the summer, we had one of the sheriff deputies come and do an on-site inspection for any of our parents who wanted one."

"Great. Can you check Hope's? I'll go get her."

They walked to Karen Hill's classroom and Hope ran to the doorway to meet them.

"Are you done already? Mrs. Hill was going to read a

story. Then we're going to draw pictures about the story and have juice and granola bars."

"I am done, pumpkin," Jared said. "You can come back tomorrow and stay all afternoon."

Hope's face crumpled, then brightened. "If you let me stay, I'll do whatever Mrs. Hill says."

Becca's throat ached. *Exactly like Ari—and me— always wanting to do things right.* No wonder Hope and Ari had become fast friends. Hope had had so much upheaval in her young life. Becca could understand her uncertainty and wanting to please others. But Ari had had a lot of constants in her life—her, the Nortons, Becca's parents and her brother and his family, even though they didn't live close by. A lot of constants until this summer, when all of a sudden Matt had decided he wanted his visitation time.

Becca stood on her toes to speak into Jared's ear so only he could hear, his clean masculine scent making her nearness to him feel more intimate than it was. "Since we have all of Hope's paperwork it would be all right for her to stay the rest of the day. I know Karen won't mind."

His warm smile of appreciation washed away most of her earlier insecurity about Ari and herself.

"Okay," he said. "You can stay. I'll pick you up at four o'clock. If you want to come home before then, ask Mrs. Hill to call me."

Hope flung herself at Jared and wrapped her arms around his legs. "I love you, Jared."

He went perfectly still and the love on his face for the little girl melted Becca to the core. Jared Donnelly had so many facets. He wasn't an easy man to know.

He lifted Hope and hugged her back. "I love you, too. Remember, Mrs. Hill will call if you need me."

"We'll be fine," Karen said. "Won't we, Hope?"

"Yep," the little girl answered.

Becca touched his arm. "This is a good time for us to slip out before Hope has a chance to change her mind."

"Maybe I should stay with her."

"No." She grabbed his arm and guided him out of the room toward the outside door. "Trust me."

His faced tensed in a tight smile.

"I know what I'm doing." Or at least she did concerning Hope.

As they walked to his truck, they passed a car Becca didn't recognize that had a bumper sticker with the awful X-ed out picture of Jared on his bike that she'd seen on the signs the protesters outside the town hall had carried. From the way Jared accelerated his pace, she knew he had, too.

He jerked open the back door of his truck and Becca recoiled, her stomach churning from the smell of stale beer that hit her.

"Awful, isn't it?"

"Yeah," she squeaked out, not sure she wanted to hear what he might say next as an excuse. She'd heard them all.

"Connor borrowed my truck to pick up a furniture donation for the fall fair. While he was at the donor's house, he talked him into donating a stash of returnable bottles the man had out in his garage along with the furniture. Connor had to put them in the backseat because the back of the truck was full of furniture. Some of the bottles weren't empty. I've tried everything Gram has suggested to get the smell out of the rug."

Now that was one excuse she hadn't heard. She wanted to trust him, believe he wasn't like Matt, wasn't like his father. But after the strain of this morning, all she could think was *I have to give Jared extra credit for creativity.*

* * *

"It's kind of like washing Dad away," Josh said Saturday evening when he and Jared went out to check on the success of the industrial-strength cleaner Josh had brought over to get the beer smell out of Jared's truck.

Jared hated to feed his brother's bitterness, but he could relate. Every time he'd opened the truck door, the smell had reminded him of their father. It was good to have it finally gone.

"Jared, Josh." Connor came of the house, letting the door slam behind him. "I need one of you to help me."

"Do what?" Josh asked first.

"Sandy Schuyler called and asked me if I'd help her track down her son, Toby. He came home last night half-drunk, and she took the keys to his pickup away, along with the fake ID she found in his jeans pocket when she threw them in the washer before work. He found them while she was at work today and took off. She called one of his friends from school, and he said he might be playing pool with some older guys Sandy doesn't like. The friend gave her the jean of a couple bars they might be at. Not places she'd want to go by herself."

"I'll come," Jared said. He had a hard time picturing the demure widowed town librarian trolling bars to find her teenage son.

"And I'll stay with Hope." Josh's voice had a tone of relief Jared couldn't quite figure.

"Yeah, thanks," Jared said.

When their brother was in the house, Connor said, "After you left, once Josh could drive, Mom used to ask him to find Dad, bring him home," Connor said. "He hated it."

As if I didn't. Jared felt a twinge of guilt that that job had fallen to Josh when he'd left. Josh seemed to have taken their father's actions and abandonment the hardest of the three of them.

"Where are we headed?" he asked as he opened the door to his truck.

"Sandy said The Road House is the most likely place."

Bile filled Jared's throat. "One of dear old Dad's favorite haunts."

He ignored Connor's sidewise glance.

"That's Toby's father's truck," Connor said as they neared The Road House.

Jared had a fleeting thought that they should have taken Connor's car. He didn't need someone seeing his truck here and reporting it to the Sheriff and Becca.

He made a sharp turn into the parking lot, parked and they went in.

"Toby," Connor said when they spotted him at the pool table.

The teen raised his cue. "Pas..." He glanced at the guys with him. "Connor, Jared."

They crossed the bar in a few strides.

Toby leaned the cue against the wall. "Ya know, Jared Donnelly, the motocross racer," he slurred to his friends, waving his arms expansively.

They nodded in Jared's direction.

"Come on, Toby," Connor said. "Time to go."

"No," he said with the petulance of a two-year-old. "I'm playing a game."

Connor touched Toby's arm and repeated, "Time to go."

Jared saw the teen start his swing at Connor before Connor did and nudged his brother out of the way, raising his forearm to deflect Toby. *Too late.* The wild roundhouse hit Jared square in the left eye. The guys with Toby snickered, and Jared had to draw on the strength of his faith to stop himself from turning on them.

Toby lost his balance, crashed into some chairs and wiped out a table full of bottles and glasses. Jared blinked his already-swelling eye and caught Connor grabbing Toby from behind as the sound of a police siren filled the bar.

Great! Someone must have called the sheriff's department. He winced, not entirely from pain. Forget someone seeing his truck in The Road House parking lot. It probably would be all around town that he'd been in a bar fight, and he'd have one beauty of a black eye to back up the gossip.

Chapter Eleven

"What happened to you?" Brendon intercepted Jared when he brought Hope to The Kids' Place the following Monday afternoon.

Jared gripped Hope's hand.

"He got a black eye helping Connor get a bad boy for his mommy," she answered for him.

Brendon bounced on his toes. "Then, what Grandpa said is true. You and Pastor Connor got in a bar fight. Cool!"

Leave it to the Paradox Lake grapevine. He should have gone to church services yesterday rather than thinking he could avoid causing gossip by keeping himself and his black eye at home.

"Brendon Michael," Becca said. "That is not cool. Go help Ms. Leanne take down the lunch tables."

No, a bar fight wasn't cool, but Becca's voice was. Beyond cool. Downright icy.

"Jared, can we talk in my office after you sign Hope in with Karen?"

"Sure." He walked Hope to her classroom and back to the Fellowship Hall feeling all the dread of a man facing death row. She couldn't hold his action against him or his racing-school project once she heard what really happened. Could she? He walked into the office, and Becca closed the door behind him.

She stood behind the desk. "Tell me it isn't true."

"It isn't true."

She narrowed her eyes and glared at him. He wondered how many years of teaching it had taken her to perfect the look.

"Can I sit?"

She nodded and remained standing.

He pulled the chair over and sat in it backward, his arms crossed on the back, forming his own line of defense. "I know it looks bad. I look bad." He gave her a slow smile he usually found to be effective in softening women's anger.

She crossed her arms and looked down at him.

Okay, if that was what she wanted. "I did get the black eye in a fight at The Road House with a seventeen-year-old kid."

"You…a seventeen-year-old…The Road House. How could you?" She spat out her words. "Kids like Brendon look up to you. And you want to run a program for teens? Hate to tell you, but that's not the way to get supporters."

"Sit down."

Her gaze burned through him.

"Please."

She sank into the chair behind the desk. "It gets worse?"

"No. Connor got a call from Sandy Schuyler about Toby. He's been hanging out with some older guys she doesn't like. He'd come home Friday night smelling of beer and she took away the keys to his pickup. He's seventeen. He was furious with her. He found the keys in her room while she was at work at the library on Saturday and was gone when she got home."

Becca placed her hand over her heart. "Poor Sandy. She's had such a hard time with Jeff's illness and death."

"She asked Connor if he would help her track Toby down. She was afraid to go after him herself, especially after the blowup they'd had the night before. And the places where she suspected she might find her son aren't exactly her usual type of hangout. Connor asked me to go with him instead."

Becca nodded.

"He was trying to reason with the kid when Toby took a swing at him. I tried to deflect it, and I did with my face."

Jared tried the slow grin again with more success. Becca's features softened with almost as much concern as she'd expressed for Sandy.

"That really is some shiner you have. Does it hurt?"

"Nah, not really." He didn't need to tell her he'd iced it numb this morning.

"What's going to happen to Toby? He was in my honors eleventh-grade history class this past year, doing really well until the Christmas break. Then his dad died. His grades and behavior both tanked after that."

Jared wondered what it would be like to have a father he'd miss like Toby obviously did his. He hadn't felt much of anything when Mom had started the proceedings to have his father declared dead so she could sell the family house in Paradox Lake.

"Toby's exactly the kind of kid I want to help. That my racing-school program could help." He searched her face and found she hadn't closed down—yet. "He needs a boot in the right direction from someone other than Sandy who, I'm sure, is grieving as much as or more than he is. And a way to vent his anger. There's nothing like a good rough ride against a little competition to drain it out of you."

"Ken said the sheriff's department was called."

His jaw tightened at her abrupt change in conversation. So much for sharing some of his vision for the school. He couldn't read her at all. When she hadn't stopped his kiss, he'd thought she was letting him into her life. A place, he'd since realized, he wanted to be. He was letting her into his. Her seemingly nothing-but-the-facts attitude cut that short.

"The Sheriff had to call and spread the good news. He can't give it up, can he?" Jared shut his mouth. He wasn't good at playing by the rules. But for Becca he could try.

"No, he keeps his finger in a lot of pies."

Including, from what he'd seen, Becca's life.

"The sheriff's deputy was really decent about not arresting Toby for disorderly conduct." *Or us.* "The bar owner decided not to press it after I told him I'd pay for any damage Toby caused. I expect when I get the bill it'll be for a considerable amount of damage."

"From one teenager swinging one punch?"

"That, and he knocked over a few chairs and smashed some bottles and glasses. He was pretty wasted. But, no, not that much damage. But I did see dollar signs in the owner's eyes when I made the offer and he realized who I was."

"Does that bother you?"

"I'd be lying if I said it didn't. But if Connor and I can get through to Toby, it'll be worth whatever the owner tries to gouge me for."

"What are you and Connor going to do?"

"The unofficial trade-off for no charges is community service for the church for the rest of the summer.

Whatever Connor thinks is fitting. We talked yesterday. Connor is going to have Toby start by filling in for the church cleaning-and-maintenance guy who takes July off as vacation. And he and I are going to rebuild the engine in his truck."

"Sandy's onboard with that? At the conference I had with her about Toby and his failing grades a few weeks before final exams, she was talking about junking the truck so it wouldn't be around for him to use to get in trouble. It's an old vehicle his father used only around the farm."

"That's the beauty of it. The truck will be out of commission indefinitely. We're going to do a painstakingly thorough job of repairing it."

Becca laughed an all-out uninhibited laugh. Then, she sobered. "Does Toby remind you of yourself?"

Jared didn't have a ready answer. He didn't know the teen well enough. All he knew was that Toby and his mother needed help.

"You couldn't have been much older than Toby when you took out the Nortons' fence."

He went numb. It always came back to the past.

"You remember that?"

"No. I was away at college. Emily told me after you'd returned."

He didn't know whether to be angry with Emily or flattered that the women had been talking about him.

"I was a little older, and had been drinking at The Road House, too. Different owners, but the place is still the same. This time, the deputy cited the owner-bartender for serving a minor. I never could figure out why Sheriff Norton never had. He ran a tight ship about everything else."

Becca flushed. "Because of Matt. He and his friends

used to get together there and have a few beers when they came home on college breaks."

Jared whistled. "I didn't think Norton would look the other way for anyone."

"He has his blind side."

Jared waited for her to elaborate. It might give him some insight into why the former sheriff had it in for him. But she didn't.

Several long seconds of tight-lipped silence ticked by. "If we're done," he said, "I'd like to get going. The afternoons when Hope is in here are my work time."

"Of course. I hope everything goes well with Toby."

Jared told himself she meant it, not that she doubted his ability to turn around the teen. He opened the office door to Brendon and two of the boys from his day-care group sauntering down the hall.

"See. I told you." Brendon pointed at his eye and continued with an admiration that made Jared sick to his stomach. "Just like the articles in the racing magazines my grandpa wouldn't buy me but I looked at in the store. Only I didn't know Jared then."

"The ones you told me about with him beating up that guy and trashing his car?" the wide-eyed kid with Brendon asked. "He did that here, too? Cool!"

Jared exploded, echoing Becca's earlier words. "No, it isn't cool. And I wasn't in a bar fight last weekend. I didn't beat anyone up. And I didn't tear any place apart."

The boys edged away from him toward the wall.

"As for the stories in the magazines." Jared swung around to face Becca. He needed to tell her this more than the boys. "I was in a bad place in my life. I did some things I'm not proud of. That incident isn't one of them. The man I tackled, not beat up, was attacking a woman in the parking lot of a restaurant. I didn't trash his car. He threw his whiskey bottle through the wind-shield himself. People should get all the facts before they spread the news."

"Boys, go back to your room," Becca said.

They sped off.

"I'm sorry," she said.

"No need. I've already asked for and received all the forgiveness I need. And to set the record straight, because I know people are talking, Hope isn't my daughter and I can prove it. But, if it makes you and everyone else happy, she could have been."

The blood drained from Becca's face, and he wanted to snatch back his words. He was angry at people thinking the worst of him, not at Becca. Instead, he chose to leave.

Jared waited until Becca's car was the only one left in the church parking lot before going into the Fellowship Hall to pick up Hope. After being a jerk the last time he and Becca had talked, he had to handle this right. It didn't help that he'd stubbornly avoided her for the rest of that week because she'd been avoiding him. And then he'd been out of town for the past few days at an alumni race with other retired motocross champions for the grand reopening of the track where he'd won his first championship. He'd missed Becca. He needed to tell her he wanted her in his life on whatever terms she was comfortable with.

He strode into the hall with a lot more confidence than he felt.

"You're back," Hope squealed.

"Sure am, pumpkin. I said I would be." He scooped the little girl up in his arms and gazed over her head at Becca.

She smiled at him, a good sign.

"And I have an invitation from Grandma Stowe for all of us to come to dinner tonight."

"Ari, too?"

"Ari, too, and Brendon and Becca."

"Can we go, Mommy?" Ari asked.

Jared searched Becca's face for any sign of disapproval of his using the kid card to get her to agree.

"I don't see why not." She put him out of his misery. "I'll close up the day care, and we'll meet you at Edna and Harry's," Becca said.

"If it's okay with Jared, could I ride with him?" Brendon asked. "You don't like to talk about motorcycles or racing, and I want to know about the race he was in this week."

"What race?"

Becca sounded bothered that he had raced.

"It was that alum, alum…"

"Alumni," Jared helped Brendon.

"Yeah. I told you about it, Mom. Remember, Ian and I watched it on the sports channel his dad gets."

"I remember. But I'd rather you ride with me."

There was the disapproval he'd dreaded when he'd walked in. Was it because of Matt and the beer smell in his truck the other week? Or did she disapprove of him talking with Brendon about bikes and racing? He knew she wanted to discourage her son's interest in motocross. Maybe she'd tell him when he got her alone, if he succeeded in getting her alone.

Grandma engineered the dinner perfectly. Whether or not Jared's plan worked, he owed her big time.

"Edna, the dinner was wonderful," Becca said when they'd all finished. "Thank you for inviting us. We had a busy day at The Kids' Place today. I wasn't looking forward to going home and having to cook dinner. Let me know if there's something I can do to reciprocate." She pushed her chair back from the table as if she were getting ready to leave.

Jared looked at his grandmother.

"It just so happens there is. I'd like you to give Jared an hour of your time to hear him out, clear the air between the two of you."

Becca tilted her head toward Grandma. That wasn't exactly what he'd asked her to say.

"Harry and I'll take the kids out to get soft-serve ice cream, so you two can have the house to yourselves."

Somehow, Grandma was sounding more matchmaker than facilitator. His heart thumped against his chest. He half expected Becca to come up with a good reason she and the kids had to go.

"All right," she relented.

Good. But he could have done without her agreement sounding as if she was accepting a crew penalty for another member's violation.

"I made some coffee," his grandmother said. "It's in the kitchen. That special kind you like, Jared. Harry and I can't drink coffee after dinner anymore. It keeps us up all night. Come on, kids." Grandma whisked them out the door.

"Want a cup?"

"Special coffee?" Becca smiled. "I thought Connor was the one who liked gourmet coffee."

"He is. But Grandma made it for us. I can't let it go to waste."

"No, we couldn't do that."

He went into the kitchen and brought back two cups of coffee on a tray with cream and sugar and honey that

Grandma had left out on the counter next to the coffee-maker. "Let's have it in the living room."

He placed the tray on the coffee table in front of the couch and motioned her to take a seat. He sat next to her.

Becca added cream and honey to hers and took a sip. "Hazelnut. But I'm sure you didn't finagle this get-together to talk about coffee."

"True. I arranged it to talk about us."

She raised an eyebrow.

He wiped his hands on his jeans. *Great*. Now, he sounded like a bad chick flick. "I'm sorry I lost my temper at the day-care center. What I have to say isn't an excuse. It's an explanation. I let what people were thinking get to me. Then, you accused me of being unfit to run a program for kids. I'm not my father. I live every day trying not to be like him."

"I know. I apologize for that." She placed her hand on his. "I had other things bothering me. I shouldn't have taken them out on you."

He flipped her hand over and entwined his fingers with hers. "The Sheriff giving you more trouble?"

She slipped her fingers from his and put her hands in her lap. Why'd he go and mention the Sheriff?

"Nothing new," she said.

"What can I do to help?" He pressed his palms to his thighs. His offer left him open to her retreating to her previous stand that they keep things between them strictly businesslike—Zoning Board petitioner to board member, parent to teacher.

"Thanks. But it's not your problem."

"I could make it my problem." That's what he'd be doing if he pursued Becca. Her kids and her ex were part of the package. He drank in her beauty and the person he was learning she was. It was definitely worth exploring, and, hey, he carried heavier baggage than she did. Besides, he might enjoy some one-on-one with the Sheriff.

She chewed her lower lip.

"Becca, I like you." He didn't care if he probably sounded like one of her high school students with a mad crush. He had to get it out. "I like spending time with you and your kids." He stopped himself from telling her how much the remark made by the woman at the soft-serve ice-cream stand about what a nice family they made had affected him. That would have been *too* sappy. "I'd like to spend more time with you."

Her shoulders sagged, and he bounced his leg in nervous anticipation.

"Oh, Jared."

A chill went through him. She was going to shoot him down. He'd had his share of brush-offs, but none of them had felt as crushing as this.

"I like you, too." Her lips curved in a wobbly smile.

He slid his arm along the back of the couch behind her.

"It's too soon."

Too soon? It had to be six or seven years since Matt had left her.

"I've been praying for direction in my life, about the kids and the Nortons, about the Zoning Board decision…" Her voice softened. "About you."

His throat clogged.

"The only answer I've gotten is 'give things time.' I think He's saying wait until after the board decision." She clasped and unclasped her hands. "I'm not always good at listening and hearing."

"I understand that. I've been known to not hear, even when He hammers the message into my head."

"That's an interesting picture. Are you saying you can be hardheaded?"

"Something like that."

"Give me until after the Zoning Board vote. You may change your mind by then." She forced a laugh. "I'm praying Matt's parents will back off, no matter how I vote. They have before. It's like they have to prove to themselves they have power. We might even be able to come to a long-term agreement outside the official agreement Matt and I have. They really do like seeing the kids, and I think they're afraid they won't after they retire to Florida. That's probably what all the pressure lately is about. Ken's just pinning it on your project."

Knowing Sheriff Norton and the way he'd always seemed to have it in for his family, Jared wasn't at all sure about that.

"So, what does that mean? Avoiding each other? That's kind of hard with Hope attending The Kids' Place and Ari being her closest friend."

"No, it means we keep things platonic." She twirled a strand of her dark hair around her finger. "You have to know, though, that no matter what happens, my kids come first."

He dropped his hand to her shoulder. "I know." He did. Hope's arrival had given him insight into a parent's love. The age difference made Hope more of a daughter to him than a sister. He wouldn't do anything that would hurt Becca or her kids.

He squeezed her to his side, and she didn't pull back. It was enough. He could wait.

"Mommy, come on. Jared is going to be here in five, no four minutes." Ari was making good use of the watch her father had bought her last week—a woman's watch that must have cost enough to buy half of the back-to-school clothes she'd need this fall. Matt would probably count the cost as child support.

She sighed. Maybe she shouldn't go look at the maple sideboard the woman who had inherited Bert's house was selling at her yard sale. But Jared had seen the sideboard and said it looked like the dining room table and chairs from her grandmother that she had in her dining room. And he'd asked the woman to let her have first look. Of course, it might not be the same at all. Jared could be using the sale to get them together, as he had the dinner at his grandmother's house. She'd thought about that and the possibility of running into her ex-in-laws at the sale and the scene that could cause. But she couldn't base her every move on what Ken and Debbie might think.

"Yeah." Brendon stuck his head in her room. "Do you really need to put on makeup and stuff? It's Saturday. I want to get to Ian's so we can go fishing while the fish are still biting."

Ari looked at her watch again. "I don't want Mrs. Hazard to leave without me and Hope." Anne Hazard was taking the three girls to the waterslide park at Lake George, while her husband was taking Ian, Brendon and their younger son on a fishing cruise.

"Guys! We could all stay home and clean the house."

That quieted them down. Becca checked her makeup in the mirror, twisted up her hair and fastened it with a barrette. Ari had a point. She usually didn't wear makeup on weekends except for church. And she'd taken more time choosing which shorts and top to wear than she would have if she'd been going to the sale alone. But, she'd admit it to herself, if not to anyone else: she wanted to look nice for Jared. Even though, at her best, a small-town high school teacher like her wasn't in the same league as the women he usually dated.

She spun away from the mirror. Today wasn't a date. They weren't dating. He'd simply offered his truck to bring the sideboard to her house if she bought it. Although she'd believed what Jared had told her at his grandmother's house, believed that's how he felt at the moment, she had doubts about her holding his interest long. He'd lived such a different life. Came from a different family background.

A cardinal chirped outside. That didn't mean she couldn't enjoy his company while he was here. She just wouldn't let her heart get involved.

"He's here," Brendon called up to her.

She smiled to herself and headed down the stairs. She didn't want to keep them waiting.

"Ready?" Jared asked as she stepped off the last stair. His warm appraisal of her said it had been worth her extra fussing.

"Yes." She picked her purse up from the end table. "A couple of us are very anxious to go places and do things with their friends."

"I know how they feel," Jared said.

They dropped the kids off at the Hazards' and drove to the yard sale. Several cars lined the road in front of the house. Jared pulled behind the last one in line. While Becca was unfastening her seat belt, he walked around and opened the cab door for her.

"Thanks." She couldn't remember the last time a man had opened a car door for her.

He shut it behind her. "We aim to please."

And he did, with his working man's tan, black T-shirt and well-worn jeans.

"Jared," a woman called across the yard.

He waved a greeting. "That's Nanci, the woman Bert

left his house to." He grabbed her hand and led her over to the porch, where Nanci was standing.

Jared introduced Becca to Nanci, who took them inside to the dining room.

"Here it is." Nanci motioned to the sideboard.

Becca ran her hand across the carved design on the front of the three drawers. "It's beautiful, and a perfect match to my dining room set."

Nanci laughed. "Glad it matches something. As you can see, it doesn't match anything in this room, or anywhere else in the house, for that matter. In fact, I don't think any three items in the house match."

Becca looked around the room and saw what she meant. Only three of the eight chairs around the dining table matched, and the china cabinet and small phone table were completely different from any of the other pieces.

"Bert was a collector," Jared said.

"You've got that right," Nanci said. "You should see the stuff out in the old horse barn. Tools, motors, who knows what else. A man's bargain paradise."

Jared's eyes lit. "Mind if I go look?"

"By all means," Nanci said.

Jared looked at Becca.

"Go ahead," she said. "I'll look around until you come back."

He was gone almost before she'd finished. Becca walked around the rest of the house, checking out what else Nanci had tagged for sale before returning to the dining room and the sideboard.

"How much?" Becca asked Nanci, testing the sideboard's three drawers and the cabinet doors.

Nanci quoted a price far below what Becca knew the

value was. "That's all?" Becca asked breaking every buyer's cardinal rule.

The woman glanced in the direction Jared had taken out of the house and shifted her weight from foot to foot. "Yes. I want to get rid of most of Bert's things so I have room for my own."

Becca touched the carved design again. "Did Jared pay you the difference between the real value of the sideboard and the price you gave me?" Her breath hitched. He didn't need to use his money to impress her.

"No." Nanci looked back and forth over her shoulders. "He tried to, but I told him that was a dumb idea and that if I did and you found out, he'd be in big trouble."

"You've got that right. So, how much do you want?"

Nanci quoted the same price. "Don't worry. I'm so thrilled Bert left me this place, I don't mind sharing my blessing. Besides, I'll make enough off the rest of the sale, probably a killing on what your man alone comes back with from the barn."

"He's not my man. He's…" What was Jared? "We're friends."

Nanci smiled. "So you're taking the sideboard?"

Becca considered the cost again. She'd taken enough money out of her school-tax savings account to cover it. And the last time she and her mother had talked, Mom had asked her what she wanted for her birthday. She and Dad would gladly give her what Nanci was charging for the sideboard.

"Sure she is. She loves it," Jared said from the doorway. He grinned at her. "I could tell by the way you kept touching it."

He was right. And she rarely did anything for herself. Becca pulled out her wallet and paid for the piece before her responsible, self-sufficient side took control again.

Jared nodded. "I'll settle up with Nanci for the stuff I want from the barn and find someone to help me carry it out to the truck."

He spread the sale tags out on the sideboard for Nanci. She totaled them on a hand calculator, showing him the result.

Becca watched wide-eyed as he peeled off at least ten one hundred–dollar bills.

"Keep the change," he said.

"Thanks."

Becca's eyes locked with Nanci's. "It's ten dollars," Nanci mouthed.

"What was that?" Jared asked when they got outside.

"Girl stuff." Becca pushed a stray strand of hair back into her barrette.

His expression clearly said he wasn't buying her answer, but he didn't press her for an explanation. He lifted his hand to shield the sun from his eyes. "I see a willing body to help me move your sideboard."

Becca followed him as he strode across the lawn to a group of young men.

Jared slapped one of them on the back. "Ah, just the man I was looking for."

Toby Schuyler turned around, giving Becca a glimpse of the two guys the teen was with. She recognized them as students she'd had several years ago, and not people Toby's mother would be happy to see him hanging with.

"Jared. I thought we were on for this afternoon, not this morning. Fixing the truck." Toby sounded like he added the last sentence for the other guys. "We were looking at the tools and stuff for sale."

"We are on for this afternoon," Jared said.

Becca watched Jared size up the other guys. They both dropped their heads at his scrutiny. More likely they were casing the barn to come back later after the sale for anything that was left.

"Later, Tobe," one of them said, and they slunk away.

"I need you to help me carry a piece of furniture to my truck for Ms. Norton."

Toby blinked as if he'd just noticed her. "Hi, Ms. Norton. Sure." His gaze shot to his friends getting in a car and roaring off.

"The sideboard is in the house," Jared said.

Becca directed the guys and the sideboard out to the truck. They lifted it into the back. Jared had bought a lot of other stuff. Things he'd use or nostalgic remembrances? Becca was discovering he had a softer side he wasn't aware of.

"You ready to work?" Jared asked Toby.

"Got nothing else to do."

"Good. We'll swing by Ms. Norton's house first to drop her off and unload the sideboard and then head over to the parsonage to work on your truck. Connor's letting us use half of the garage as our work space," Jared said for her benefit.

Becca bit back a smile at the grimace Toby made at Jared's explanation. Jared had a talent for getting in the heads of kids. The teen would have a tough time sneaking out with the vehicle if it was in the parsonage garage.

Half an hour later, Becca was standing in her dining room admiring the sideboard and how well it went with the rest of her dining room set. Whether intentionally or not, Jared had given her an out by planning to work on the truck with Toby. She hadn't had to come up with a good reason they couldn't spend the afternoon together. She should have been thankful. So why was she peeved at him?

Chapter Twelve

She couldn't believe the Nortons would do this to her. Becca held the letter from Family Court in her shaking hand, glad, for once, that the kids were at Matt's. They were taking her to court. And here she'd been foolish enough to think she had things under control with him and his parents. Apparently, it didn't matter that she'd done almost everything they'd asked concerning the kids, including hiding her feelings for Jared. Who did they think they were?

Becca collapsed on the couch. Better question. Who was she to allow them to do this to her? Not the parent she was trying to be. Ari's sad face when she'd asked last night if she *had* to go to her father's again wouldn't leave her head.

Matt had called Wednesday night, saying he "needed" the kids this weekend. Evidently, his boss had invited him and his family to his summer home on the shore, and Matt thought it would look bad if he didn't have the kids. She'd felt she had to say yes. He was supposed to have had them last weekend when she went to the estate sale but hadn't taken them. And now he was suing her for custody.

She kicked off her flip-flops and pulled on her athletic shoes. She had to get out of the house or she'd explode.

Picking up speed across the meadow, she ran until her lungs burned. At the sound of an engine, she slowed her pace until she could stop. Bending over, she rested her hands on her thighs and slowed her breathing. When she'd caught her breath, she straightened and looked out over the meadow toward her house. Jared was speeding around the perimeter of his property. At least she thought it was Jared. But he wasn't riding his green street bike. She watched the rider circle around toward the road. He turned and roared down the hill, flying over the gully. Her breath caught until he landed perfectly on the other side. The way the rider melded with his vehicle, it had to be Jared.

He curved around again in a tight circle, seemingly oblivious to her and everything else and started weaving a figure eight. As he completed his second pass, he raised his hand in a wave, grabbed hold of the hand grip again and gunned the engine. Watching him barrel toward her, she relived her ride home with him on the bike, the exhilaration, the feeling of power and freedom. Jared finished with a fifty-foot wheelie that ended a few feet to her left. He tore off his helmet and grinned.

"Show-off."

"It's what I've spent years getting paid to do."

"And you loved it."

He turned sheepish. "Yeah, I did." He swung off the bike and laid it down. "No kickstands on racers," he explained.

"Are you going to miss it badly?"

He shrugged. "I can do exhibitions to scratch the itch."

"Like the race last week? Brendon said you won."

"Exactly." He grinned again. "But I don't need the

validation of cheering crowds and winning anymore. I haven't in a while. And once the track's built, I'll be racing with the kids. I think I'll get a lot more satisfaction from that. If I need more excitement, I can come over and race for myself whenever the track isn't in use. One of the perks of being the owner."

Jared spoke as if the racing school and track were a done deal. Confidence spurred by his ride, or did he know something she and the Zoning Board didn't know yet?

"I know the school is an off subject between us, and I'm not trying to sway your vote." He ran his hand over his already-tousled hair. "But I have some information from GreenSpaces that might interest you. Anne's sent it to Tom."

Becca sucked in a breath and released it slowly. "I'd like to hear it." *Especially if it will help me vote in good conscience for the track and against the Sheriff.*

"The DOT came through with its report. Its engineers have recommended a way of rerouting traffic to bypass Conifer Road altogether and lessen the potential traffic on Route 9."

"No roundabout?" she asked.

"No roundabout. And I'm working with the Girl Scout Council to donate some of my property to make a bigger buffer between the track property and the camp."

"That's great. It resolves two of your opposition's major points of contention, the reasonable opposition, that is." Excitement for Jared bubbled up inside her. Without thinking, she threw her arms around his neck.

He dropped his hands to her waist and tilted his head. "I know I'm not supposed to do this." He lowered his lips to hers.

"No, you're not." She accepted his kiss, leaning into

the solid wall of his chest. But anything that felt this right couldn't be all wrong.

Too soon, he lifted his head, bringing her back to reality. He gazed down at her with a softness in his eyes that contrasted sharply with the angular features of his face and masculine stubble of a beard that shadowed his chin. A softness that empowered her and made her believe that by relying on God's direction and with Jared's strength supporting her emotionally, she could stand up to anything Matt and his parents could throw at her.

She was so beautiful, with her dark hair gleaming in the sun and a hint of a blush on her cheeks. The untouchable Becca Morgan Norton in his arms.

He swallowed the lump in his throat. "I've wanted to do that again."

"Me, too," she said, her voice as wispy as the summer breeze passing over the meadow.

Her brown eyes misted, dulling the euphoria that had filled him when she hadn't stopped his kiss.

"But it doesn't change things," she said.

He lifted his finger and wiped the tear that ran down her cheek. Another followed it. *Nice work, Donnelly.* He couldn't leave well enough alone. "What's wrong?"

"Everything." She buried her face in his chest.

He hesitantly smoothed his hand over her hair. He'd thought things were looking up for him, for both of them.

She stepped away and rubbed her palms over her cheeks. "It's not you, this." She dropped her hands in an open-armed gesture. "Us." She crossed her hands on her chest and took a deep breath. "Matt's suing for custody of Ari and Brendon and permission to move them to Florida. My mind is such a jumble. One minute I think

I can handle him and his parents, that I have everything under control. The next…"

Jared bit back a word he shouldn't say. "After the way the Sheriff and his wife treat you and all of the hoops you've jumped through for them and Matt, he's suing you for custody? On what grounds? Your kids couldn't ask for a better mother."

She gave him a watery smile. "Thanks. As the saying goes, you can sue anyone for anything. It doesn't mean you're going to win."

"I'm not part of this, am I?" He had to ask.

"No, not specifically." She rushed on before he could ask her to clarify that. "Matt and his attorney are contending that Matt and Crystal have a more stable *two-parent* household. Crystal doesn't work outside the home. He makes a comfortable living."

"What century are they coming from? If that's their tack, how do they justify him not sharing that comfortable living more equally with you for the kids? Gram told me about your need to work this summer. I can't imagine it's for things for you."

Becca raised her hand to halt him. "Matt also accuses me of using my nonwork time for socializing rather than spending time with Brendon and Ari, of dumping them with Ken and Debbie. That's ironic considering Brendon and Ari complain that Matt isn't home or is entertaining clients at the house half of the time when they're there and that Crystal constantly tells them to go play or watch TV in their rooms."

Jared clenched his hands into tight fists. It was an unchristian thought, but he'd like to break something or someone.

"I thought Debbie and Ken liked to watch the kids for me. They always asked for Matt's weekends before Matt started using his visitation rights this summer." She threw up her hands. "And where do I socialize? I sometimes go to the once-a-month meeting of the Singles Group at church. Last year I chaired the Career Day at school. That required me to attend a few evening meetings. And I've been to two Zoning Board meetings." She laughed a harsh laugh. "After the Sheriff suggested I fill the vacancy on the board."

"When did he suggest you join the board?" he demanded.

"Shortly before the meeting where the board decided that we needed a public hearing before we could vote on your project."

His chest tightened. "The timing. It has to be at least partly about me or about getting back at my family and me. Ken Norton has always disliked us. I suspect it's something between him and Dad." He ran his finger down her cheek. "You know I wouldn't intentionally do anything to hurt you or Brendon and Ari."

"I know." She hung her head and shook it.

Her defeat fueled his anger. "What about Matt's drinking, that you suspect he's abusing alcohol when the kids are with him? Equal game. I know the Sheriff is using my supposed alcohol use against me, talking up that I'm just like my father to anyone who'll listen. The gossip paints you, too, if you associate with me."

"No, I can't go there." She stood ramrod straight. "I have the information about Matt's drinking only from Brendon. I won't make him speak against his father, even if it's only to the court-appointed law guardian to share with the court. I'd rather he and Ari not be dragged into it at all. Nor should they have to. It's highly unlikely the judge will act on revoking my custody. Besides, Matt and Crystal don't want the kids there full-time. He as much as told me so. It would interfere with their life-style. We'll end up taking up the court's time to work out a new visitation agreement to accommodate Matt and Crystal's move, something we could sit down with our lawyers and do."

"So taking you to court is all a power trip."

"Pretty much. Matt and the Sheriff revel in the grand-standing, being in charge."

"In their minds."

Becca frowned.

He shouldn't have been so caustic. Jared knew Becca had been through this before. More than once. But it seemed like she was ready to roll over and give in to the Nortons again.

"It's so wearing on me and hard on Ari and Brendon. They hear everything from their father and grandparents as if it's a done deal, and come back to me confused and upset. I thought we had everything worked out the last time we went to court. It's been three years. Why now, again?"

"Because of Matt's move to Florida?"

"I don't know. It started earlier in the summer, before Matt got the offer in Florida."

All feeling drained from Jared. *Earlier in the summer. Like when I returned to Paradox Lake.* The last thing he wanted was to cause problems for Becca, to be respon-sible in any way for placing her in a position where she'd have to fight to keep Brendon and Ari.

Becca looked toward her house. "I need to get going. Since the kids are at Matt's, I volunteered to help Karen shop and set up for your grandmother's surprise birth-day luncheon at church tomorrow during coffee hour. I ran out to blow off some steam. I didn't intend to be gone so long."

"I can give you a lift." He nodded at his bike.

"You only have one helmet."

"You can wear it. I trust myself to get us up the hill to your house safely."

"I didn't mean…"

"I'm teasing," he said, adjusting the strap on the helmet before handing it to her.

"I am a little nervous," she admitted. "I've only ridden a motorcycle once, with you, on the road."

"Hey, I'm a professional. And, truth be told, the ground is more forgiving than the pavement."

She gave him a mock-stern look. "Nothing tricky on the way."

"Nothing tricky on the way," he echoed. "I promise."

He lifted his bike upright and seated himself, steadying the vehicle for Becca to climb on behind him. She slid her arms around his waist, his abs tightening at the touch of her fingers. He could get used to this.

"Hang on." He turned on the engine and took off in low gear, holding the bike back. As he'd said, he'd never do anything to hurt her.

Jared came to a slow stop in her driveway in front of the garage and glanced up the road, half expecting the Nortons to arrive as they had the last time he and Becca had run into each other in the meadow. He shook off the bad memories, clamped his hands tighter on the grips than necessary and planted his booted feet on the driveway so she could climb off.

Becca released him and took off the helmet. She walked to the front of the bike, grinned and placed it on his head. A warmth that had nothing to do with the summer morning filled him as she adjusted the strap under his chin and snapped it to the helmet. He smiled as she ran her finger between the strap and his chin, testing the fit.

When she was satisfied, she stepped back. "Thanks for listening to me. I know it's not your problem. See you at church tomorrow."

He sat with the bike off until she was in the house. She was wrong there. It was his problem because he was part of the cause. He cranked on the motor and jetted back over the fields to the pull-in where he'd parked his truck and trailer. And he was going to do something about it.

As he slammed the door of the trailer shut behind his bike, Jared looked up at the cloudless sky. *Lord, this may be the hardest and most selfless thing I've ever done. I won't come between Becca and her children. Please give me the strength to leave Becca before I'm too in love with her to go.*

Shopping and setting up for the luncheon didn't take nearly as much time as Becca had expected. She'd had plenty of time to do all her weekend chores as well. With the kids gone to Matt's so much this summer, the house had never been cleaner—or emptier. The letter from Family Court shouted at her every time she walked by the bill-and-mail holder by the telephone in the dining room. She'd talk with Matt on Monday after the kids were back with her.

Restless energy sent her back to her summer to-do list pinned to the cork board above the stand. Most of the remaining things were outdoor tasks, and the brilliantly clear morning had given way to clouds and showers off and on. Her gaze went to the sideboard she'd bought last weekend. Cleaning it out and polishing it would kill some time. Then, maybe she'd call Emily and see if she wanted to catch whatever was showing at the Strand this week.

They could ask Tessa Hamilton to join them for coffee or something after she finished showing the film. Make it a girls' night out.

Emily picked up Becca's call on the first ring with a breathless, "Hello."

"Hi, it's Becca. I was wondering if you're up for a girls' night out tonight."

"No, sorry. One of Drew's campers had to come today instead of tomorrow. We're heading down to Albany to pick her up at the bus station. Long story. Her mother only bought her a ticket to Albany, rather than to Schroon Lake."

"Okay. I'll talk to you later." Becca hung up and tapped her contact list. Connor's name showed second on the list. She could call Jared, include Connor and Tessa in the movie invitation, as if it was a group get-together.

She clicked off her phone in disgust. What was she, one of her sophomore students with a mad crush on a senior, conniving ways to be in the same place her crush was? This morning notwithstanding, she and Jared had agreed to put off any exploration of a relationship until after the Zoning Board vote, when she'd thought the Sheriff would back off scrutinizing her every move. Now she had the Family Court hearing. Ken would still be watching. She massaged her temples. But hadn't God led her to Jared's strength? Or was she once again misreading the direction, imposing her own desire to be with Jared over His words?

Becca eyed the sideboard. Some good hard work might help her clear her mind and open it to His guidance. *Where to start?* She lined up her cleaning supplies and lemon oil on the table with a pan of warm water. Might as well begin with the drawers. She opened the first one, drew it all the way out and emptied the dirt and dust in the waste basket before gently scrubbing it clean. She did the same with the second one. Once she had them done, she'd spread the lemon oil over the wood, as she'd seen her grandmother do.

The third drawer stuck about halfway. She pulled harder, and it came out with the crunch of crumpling paper. Becca peered into the sideboard. It looked like an envelope. It must have slipped between the side of the drawer and the sideboard. She opened the door below the drawer and crouched to remove the yellowed envelope. A piece of paper with writing on it showed through the tear the drawer had ripped open. It must be a letter. Becca stood and moved to toss the envelope in the wastebasket. She stopped. The sideboard was at least one hundred years old, possibly older. The matching pieces Becca's grandmother had given her had belonged to Becca's great-grandmother. Her history teacher persona took over. The letter might have historical significance. Maybe a letter from a World War I soldier to his sweetheart.

A closer look told Becca her imagination was getting away from her. The envelope wasn't yellowed. It was yellow. Several months ago the Paradox Lake General Store had gotten an order of multi-colored envelopes that hadn't sold. At the end, the store owner had reduced the price to almost nothing. Bert had probably taken advantage of the bargain. Again, she went to throw the envelope out. The letter could be one Bert had written but hadn't been able to mail before he got so sick. She pulled out the page. An early June date was written in the top right hand corner and Jared's name was in the salutation. She should put it back in the envelope and give it to Jared. As she started to fold the letter closed, her ex-father-in-law's name, followed by Jared's father's name, drew her attention. She sat in one of the dining room chairs and smoothed out the page on the table.

When she'd finished the letter, she stared at the shaky scribbled writing. *Unbelievable.* Outrage and compassion for Jared and his family washed away the guilt she'd felt when she'd started reading. Wait until she showed it to Jared. But that would be after she confronted the Sheriff.

A few hours later, the sideboard was clean and oiled until it glistened in the late afternoon sun that streamed through the bay window. While she'd worked, Becca had thanked the Lord more than once for leading her to the letter, and she'd gone over Bert's words in her head until she was ready for the Sheriff's arrival. A car door slammed outside, pulling her from her inspection of the restored sideboard.

Becca got to the kitchen door just before Ari burst in followed by Brendon and their grandparents. "Hi, guys. Did you have a good time?"

Both kids glanced back at the Sheriff and Debbie.

"I guess," Ari said.

"Sure." Brendon shrugged.

"Well, I have a little surprise for you," Becca said with forced cheerfulness. "Your grandmother is going to take you to the soft-serve ice-cream stand."

Debbie looked over the kids' heads at Becca, clearly confused. "Ken and I were going right home. We hadn't planned on ice cream."

"What's this about?" the Sheriff demanded.

"You and I need to talk privately."

"Is this about the Family Court letter?"

Ari pressed herself to Becca's side, and Becca wrapped her arm around her daughter's shoulder. Brendon stared at the floor.

"Ken. The kids," Debbie said, her gaze darting from Ari to Brendon.

"That's between you and Matt," he said, ignoring his wife's warning.

Becca straightened to her full height. "No, we need to talk about another letter, a letter Bert Miller wrote."

The Sheriff stiffened. "Debbie, take the kids for ice cream."

"Come on, Ari, Brendon," she said without question, pushing the screen door open.

Ari looked up at Becca. The distress in her eyes took a chink out of Becca's bravado. "Go, ahead. It's okay," she said.

"Yeah," Brendon said. "Grandma's going to take us to get ice cream so Mom can talk some grown-up stuff with Grandpa."

Becca gave silent thanks for her son's perceptiveness and help with his sister.

The Sheriff stared at her narrowed eyed until the sound of Debbie starting the car filtered in to the house. "So, Donnelly got the letter."

"You know about the letter?"

"Bert threatened he was going to write Donnelly. What did he tell you it says?"

"Let's sit." Becca motioned him to the table. "Jared didn't tell me anything. I found the letter in the sideboard I bought from the woman who inherited his house."

"The house that was supposed to be Debbie's and mine." The Sheriff gripped the edge of the table. "You haven't told Donnelly?"

"No."

"Good. I'll take the letter and make the Family Court hearing go away."

"Are you trying to bribe me?"

"No," he blustered. "Matt and Crystal are having second thoughts about Brendon and Ari being with them all of the time. He has a lot of business commitments."

"And they might get in the way?"

"I didn't say that. Now, give me the letter."

The edge in the Sheriff's voice sent a ripple of fear through Becca. She drew on her inner strength to continue. "No, I'm not going to. It's all true, isn't it?"

"I can't tell you whether or not it's true if I don't know what it says. Let me look at it." He held his hand out for the letter.

Becca ignored him. "You arrested Jared's father and let him be charged and convicted of vehicular assault for running a stop sign, plowing into Liz Whittan's car and putting her in a wheelchair for life, when you knew he didn't do it."

"That's ridiculous."

"You didn't know that Bert was driving the car, not Jared's father?"

"No!"

"Then why did Bert think you did? In the letter, he apologized to Jared, saying he lied to you and you lied for him."

"That's not the way it was." The Sheriff's bluster drained away. "I didn't know before Jerry, Jared's father, was convicted. When I got to the scene, both men were out of the car. It was Jerry's car. Bert said Jerry was driving, and Jerry didn't say otherwise." The Sheriff rubbed his chin. "Jerry was really out of it. He didn't say much of anything when I arrested him, or later. You have to understand. There was bad blood between us. He stole the girl I was going to marry, Jared's mother, Gail. We went together all through high school and had an understanding. Jerry made her life torture."

Becca didn't know what to say. The Sheriff was holding a grudge for something that happened more than thirty-five years ago. He and Debbie had been married—happily, she'd thought—for thirty-five years.

"Don't look at me like that. I love Debbie. But that doesn't mean I forgot Gail or have to forgive Jerry."

"When did you know Bert was driving?"

"Not for sure until the week he died. I went with Debbie to visit him, and he told me he'd written the letter to Jared. I suspected Bert might have been a few months after Jerry was released from jail when Bert told Debbie he'd written a will giving her most of his property. She's his cousin, was his closest living relative. But they've never been close. Bert made an off-hand comment that I took to mean he was making her his heir because he thought I'd known he was driving and had kept my mouth shut.

"So Debbie knows?"

"No." A note of fear showed in his voice. "She was in the kitchen putting away the groceries we'd picked up for him. You've got to understand what it would do to me, my reputation, if this gets out."

"Like you considered what you've been doing to Jared?"

The Sheriff avoided her gaze. "Everything started falling apart when Bert died. Instead of Debbie inheriting Bert's property, most of it went to the Donnellys and that home-health aide. We'd planned on that money for our retirement. And I was afraid you wouldn't let us see the kids once we'd retired to Florida."

Disgust roiled inside Becca. And to think she'd once tried to love this man as a father.

"Donnelly showed up and it became apparent he hadn't received Bert's letter. I thought I could discredit him and he'd go away and make plans to build his race-track somewhere else before Bert's letter caught up with him. Bert and Jerry are both gone. No harm, no foul."

She stared at him in disbelief. "You saw no harm to the Donnellys? What were you thinking?"

He cleared his throat and dropped his head to his chest. "I wasn't. I was reacting. I wanted to get Debbie down to Florida so that she'd be spared some of the shame if Donnelly decided to come back later and make a big deal about it."

At least he cared something about someone else. No, that wasn't entirely fair. He loved the kids in his own way.

"You're going to tell Donnelly." It was a statement, not a question.

"Yes." She reached out to him. "But I won't keep Ari and Brendon from you. They like doing things with you and Debbie." She hesitated and then went on, "It's Matt and Crystal that they aren't crazy about spending time with." Becca braced herself for the Sheriff's blast. She'd insulted Matt, his pride and joy.

"I know. The Family Court petition was Debbie and my idea, so we'd be able to see the kids after we move. I'll get Matt to drop it."

"Thank you. You and Debbie and I can get together and work out a visitation agreement."

"You'd do that for us? You forgive me?"

"I'm doing it for Brendon and Ari, and I'll work on the forgiveness. But I think you have a few others you have to ask for forgiveness. And I trust you'll talk with Debbie?"

He blanched and nodded.

Becca heard the slam of the kitchen screen door snapping shut and breathed a calming breath.

"Mommy." Ari raced into the dining room. "Grandma

let me get a double chocolate-vanilla swirl." The evidence of the treat showed on the little girl's hands and T-shirt.

"Thanks, Debbie."

Her ex-mother-in-law's forehead wrinkled in question. "You're welcome."

The Sheriff dragged himself from his chair, showing every year of his age and then some. "We'd better get going." He and Debbie left.

"You guys need to go get ready for bed, but give me a hug first."

Ari rushed over and flung her arms around Becca. Brendon gave her a tolerant look and allowed her to hug him. When had he gotten so grown up?

While the kids were upstairs, Becca called Jared, first on his cell phone. It went right to his voice mail. More often than not, there wasn't any service at the church or parsonage. She couldn't wait to talk with him, to tell him her prayers had been answered. She dialed the parsonage's landline. The phone rang a few times and went to Connor's voice mail. She left a message for Jared to call her, knowing she probably wouldn't be able to sleep a wink tonight without talking to him.

Chapter Thirteen

He was a coward. But a coward for a good reason. He wouldn't jeopardize Becca's custody of Brendon and Ari. Jared flicked the directional on his bike and hand signaled for the exit to the hotel outside of Albany where he'd made a room reservation last night. Fortunately for him, the person taking the reservation was a fan, and he'd been able to arrange an eight o'clock check-in.

Jared had gotten home before Connor yesterday evening and played the voice mail, deleting Becca's message. That didn't stop it from bouncing around in his head. She had sounded so happy. She had something important to tell him. When they'd last talked she had been so furious with her ex-in-laws and Matt that he was certain she was going to tell him that she'd dropped her opposition to his racing school, no matter about the Family Court petition. His heart broke in a million pieces. If she'd do that for him, he could do what he now realized he had to do. Leave Paradox Lake and get out of her life. He prayed Becca would see that it would be best for everyone.

Once he was in his hotel room, he called his brother.

Connor picked up immediately. "Hey, you sure were out of here early. I didn't even hear you leave."

"Yeah. I have unexpected business in Albany." He wasn't lying. Until he'd made his decision last night, he hadn't expected to be meeting with his attorney this morning. "Can you tell Hope I'm out of town on business, like I was for the race, and I'll call her every day until I get back?"

"Every day? Reminder, Bro, you have your public hearing tomorrow night. Whatever other business you have, I can't believe you'd forgotten that."

Jared clenched his jaw. He was trying to do exactly that. Forget the whole Paradox Lake project and his plans to settle there. And it wasn't easy. Not when Becca kept appearing in his mind, her eyes dewy from their kiss the other afternoon in the meadow.

"Wait," Connor said. "Hope just got up. You can talk to her yourself."

"Hi, Jared."

"Hi, pumpkin."

"Where are you? Aren't you taking me to The Kids' Place today?"

"No, I had to go on a business trip. Connor will take you."

"You *are* coming back?"

Jared's heart constricted. Hope had lost so many people close to her. "Of course I'm coming back, in a couple days. Remember how I went to the race a couple of weeks ago? Like that."

"But I didn't get to kiss you goodbye."

"Tell you what. You can send me a kiss over the phone and I'll send you one back."

Hope made a loud smacking sound that Jared duplicated. "Tell Connor that I'll call him later."

"Okay. Will you bring me a present like you did last time?"

"Yes, I'll bring you a present. Bye-bye." He hung up and powered off his cell phone. He'd clue his brother in to his plans later. And Hope. He had to take care explaining to her that he was moving to Albany. She was better off in Paradox Lake, where she had friends and Connor and Josh. Connor was the one who wanted marriage and family, and probably had the best shot at doing that. He was less damaged than Jared and Josh. Albany was only an hour and a half away. He could zip up to see her almost anytime. After fifteen years of thinking mainly of himself, it was time he put others first.

The afternoon meeting with Dan went perfectly from a business perspective. Not only had the attorney worked all weekend scouting potential properties, but he'd also lined up a couple of potential investors in the racing school. They were going to meet with them tomorrow morning, and he had set up appointments with a real estate agent to view some houses and condos tomorrow afternoon and evening. He needed something to do to keep his mind off the public hearing he wouldn't be attending tomorrow evening.

Knowing Connor would be picking up Hope from The Kids' Place about now, he called the house and left a message for him and Hope before heading down to the hotel fitness center. He hoped it had some heavy weights he could use to work off his restlessness. He had no idea taking the right actions could feel so wrong.

Where was he? Becca looked out over the fast-filling town hall meeting room. Jared's lawyer sat at the front table without Jared. The exuberance she'd woken up with Monday morning knowing she was free to vote her conscience for the racing school tonight, had diminished with each unanswered call she'd made and text she'd sent to

Jared. Connor didn't seem to know what was going on with his brother, either, other than Jared had gone to Albany on business yesterday. As a last resort, she stooped to talking with Hope. All she'd gotten from the little girl was that Jared would be home in a couple days, like before, and was bringing her a present. Concern choked her. Jared wouldn't miss the meeting. It was too important.

Tom Hill banged his gavel on the dais. "Everyone take a seat. I'm calling this public hearing to order." Tom went through the formalities of getting the hearing under way. "So that everyone gets their say tonight, we're limiting each speaker to no more than ten minutes. The first person on the list is Eli Peyton. Eli, are you here?"

Eli rose from a chair in the center of the room and made his way to the microphone set up in the front. "I support Jared Donnelly's racing school as a teacher and guidance counselor and as a parent," he began before going on to list all of his reasons and explaining how he saw the racing program as a potential resource for troubled students.

"Thank you, Eli," Tom interrupted. "The secretary says your time is up."

Emily's husband, Drew, spoke next about how the racing program could be integrated with the summer camp sessions and other activities he offered at Sonrise Camp and Conference Center. Liz Whittan followed, rolling her wheelchair up the narrow center aisle between the rows of chairs. She ended her short statement with, "Jared Donnelly is not his father." Applause rippled across the room, punctuated with a couple of boos.

When the room quieted, Tom called the next person on the list. One of Becca's Conifer Road neighbors strode to the microphone. "The endorsements from the teachers and youth workers are fine and good, but we still have some unanswered questions about traffic congestion and the proximity of the racetrack to Camp Northern Lights."

Anne Hazard stood. "I can answer your questions, if that's agreeable with Jared's representative."

Jared's attorney rose and turned to the crowd. "That won't be necessary. Jared is considering another location and directed me to withdraw his zoning request if he wasn't here by seven-thirty." Dan nodded to the clock on the wall above the dais. "It's seven-forty-five. He must have decided on the other location."

A buzz went through the room before it settled to almost dead silence. Becca clenched her folded hands in front of her until her fingers hurt, her temperature rising with her fury. Jared hadn't said a word about that Saturday. How could he abandon his project, his dream—and her? Where was his strength to confront his foes, the strength she'd drawn on to muster enough of her own to challenge the Sheriff?

"Maybe he ran into traffic," she blurted. "Can't you call him?"

Everyone's attention turned to her. She straightened and held her head up high.

"No need." Jared's voice came from the doorway to the hall, saving her from whatever spontaneous reaction she might have exhibited next.

Her pulse quickened as he threaded his way to the front of the room, eschewing the microphone. "If it's all right with the board, I'll answer your question."

"Go ahead," Tom said.

"But first, I *was* going to withdraw the project. My attorney found me another property in the Albany area that may be better suited than my property here, and supporters, people who want to invest with me, in fact."

The crowd murmured.

"And thinking about that offer early this evening is what changed my mind. The people in Albany want to help build my racing school as a financial investment." He looked pointedly at Eli, Drew, Liz and others, ending with Becca.

She met his gaze with an equally pointed one.

"The people here..."

Was that a crack she heard in his deep voice?

"The people here who support the school support it as an investment in our community."

At least three-quarters of the room roared in approval. Becca had to grab the sides of her seat to stop herself from joining a small, but loud standing ovation.

Jared raised his hand to quiet his supporters so he could respond to the man at the microphone. "Addressing your concerns about traffic, the Department of Transportation and GreenSpaces have come up with a resolution that should relieve most people's unease. Traffic will be rerouted to bypass Conifer Road. No roundabout will be needed. We have maps available for inspection. And I'm donating land to Camp Northern Lights to buffer it from the racing school and track. Does that answer your question?"

"Yes."

"Anything else?"

"No. Thank you." Becca's neighbor returned to his seat, and Jared took the chair next to his attorney.

Tom ran through the rest of the speaker list, and Becca watched with admiration as Jared fielded questions from both supporters and opponents. While confidence wasn't something she'd ever seen lacking in Jared, he had a different way about him tonight, more at peace with himself.

"We're down to the last speaker on the list," Tom said. He called one of the Sheriff's close friends.

The man stood. "I've given my time to Ken Norton."

Jared drew his lips into a hard line that made Becca's stomach churn. What was Ken doing? She thought they'd agreed he would lay off Jared. Although, thinking back, all she remembered him actually saying was that he'd get Matt to withdraw the Family Court petition. The one thing she did know was that she was done kowtowing to the Sheriff. Whatever he might say against Jared, she was prepared to defend him.

Jared avoided her gaze and tapped his fingertips together in a tent in front of him, any remnants of the earlier peace she'd seen gone.

"As most of you know, I've been vehemently opposed to this project from the start."

Becca's shoulders tightened. She braced herself for the worse.

The Sheriff glanced over his shoulder at her and back at the crowd. "None of that opposition came from anything to do with the project itself. But I don't need to go into that here. I've done some hard thinking. The project itself is a good one. Good for our kids. Good for our community. It's something we should all get behind."

Jared dropped both hands to the table with a slap that garnered a startled look from his attorney. Sheriff Norton had just endorsed his project. In public. He looked up at Becca. She had a silly grin on her face. What was going on?

He asked Dan if they could request a short break, his mind racing over who he might be able to corner for information. Not Becca. That could be a conflict of interest for her. Not the Sheriff. On general principles, he couldn't bring himself to ask him.

Before Dan could gain recognition to request the

break, Tom asked the board for a motion to vote on the variance. The motion was made and seconded. He'd have to wait for any information.

Tom cast his vote in favor and polled the four other members in order of tenure. The secretary voted with Tom. The next member voted against. Two for, one against.

Jared rubbed the back of his neck as he watched Becca nibble her lower lip. As the newest member, she had the last and possibly deciding vote. He couldn't read her uncertainty. Was she still undecided, or contemplating what voting him down would do to them? No way after their evening at his grandmother's house could she claim there wasn't any them.

"Bob?" Tom addressed the next board member, a friend of the Sheriff. "No." He glared at the Sheriff, who glared back stony-faced.

It was up to Becca. Jared offered up a short prayer, not for her vote, but for them. He loved her. He could build his school near Albany and run it from Paradox Lake. None of his reasons for the school, except helping kids somewhere, mattered anymore.

"Becca?"

Jared's heart leaped to his throat.

"Yes," she said loud and strong, a nanosecond after Tom spoke her name.

He jumped to his feet and whooped, as much for the spark of joy he saw in Becca's eyes when she cast her vote as for his project's approval.

"We did it," Dan said, offering his hand in congratulations.

"Uh, yeah. Thanks, man. I've got to do something. I'll talk to you tomorrow." He left Dan sitting at the table and bounded up to the dais to catch Becca.

"We've got to talk," he said.

"I should say so."

Her stern teacher voice set him on edge. He was almost glad to have the Sheriff push through the crowd of people wanting to congratulate him and appear at his side. He knew how to deal with the Sheriff.

"Congratulations, Donnelly." The Sheriff's words had the same edge to them he always used when talking to Jared. "Becca, Debbie and I will keep the kids overnight, so you two can straighten things out."

The Sheriff eyed him with what Jared would take as fear in anyone else. Things were getting curiouser and curiouser, to quote the abridged version of *Alice in Wonderland* that he'd read to Hope.

"Thanks, Ken," she said. "I appreciate it."

"Where do you want to talk?" Jared asked in a voice pitched low to keep their business as private as he could with a crowd of people closing in on him.

"Go ahead and accept your congratulations, and meet me at my house afterward."

If it had been up to him, he would have skipped the congratulations, but tonight he was following Becca's lead. He accepted all the slaps on the back and handshakes with the composure his former publicist had drilled into him for public appearances, all the time wanting to blow them all off, jump on his bike and race to Becca's. Despite his best efforts to move through the crowd, it was nearly an hour later when he finally pulled in her driveway.

Jared took the steps to her kitchen door two at a time to find a note taped to the door that said, "I'm on the back deck." He tore it off and marched around back to tell her how dangerous putting the note there was, even in Paradox Lake. Anyone driving up to the house could have seen it. He rounded the corner of the house and saw her sitting in one of two matching lounge chairs. The way the moon cast a glow on her mesmerized him and drove away all inclination to reproach her.

"Jared," she said. "I wondered if you'd decided not to come."

"There were a lot of people, you know, wanting to congratulate me," he replied, still stunned by the way the moonlight highlighted her perfection. He walked up the deck steps and lowered himself into the other lounge chair.

"It looks like you and your school are on your way to success."

Did Becca think that's what the school was about, success, another trophy on his shelf? "The school won't be a success until we have some graduates prove it a success. It's for the kids, not for me."

"Not a little for you?" she goaded him.

"Some for me, I guess." He gazed at the stars in the inky background of the night sky. He could admit it to Becca. "To feed my pride in what I've accomplished with my life. To prove to the people here and to myself that I'm not like my dad. And to rebuild my family's tarnished reputation as a gesture to Josh and Connor and Mom for essentially abandoning them for my race career."

"Then why did you abandon your brothers and Hope and us yesterday?"

She wasn't making things easy for him.

"For you. I meant it when I said that I'd never intentionally hurt you. You got the letter from Family Court. I thought my being here was hurting you and the kids, that staying here would only make it worse." He swallowed. "I was falling in love with you. What I feel for you, I've never felt for any other woman. I thought I'd better leave,

leave you alone before it got to the point where I couldn't leave." His heart pounded against the wall of his chest. "But it was too late. I wasn't falling in love with you. I am in love with you."

Becca looked at him but didn't say anything. His heart felt as if it was going to explode. He didn't want to hear her say she didn't feel the same. So, before she could he said the first thing that came to mind.

"So, what's with the Sheriff?"

If she hadn't still been processing Jared's declaration, Becca would have laughed at his sudden change of subject. He loved her. But the information in Bert's letter, Jared's reaction to it, could change the situation, make it impossible to build a successful relationship, despite their shared love. *Yes.* She loved him, had given up trying to fight it. She wasn't going to share that, though, not until she knew they had a chance at a future. Why give Jared false hope?

Becca retrieved Bert's letter from the table next to her chair. "Read this."

Jared unfolded the sheet and she watched his gaze travel down the letter.

"Where did you get this?"

"I found it in the sideboard. It looked like it had slipped between one of the drawers and the wall of the sideboard before Bert could have someone mail it for him."

"So the Sheriff knew my father wasn't driving and let him go to jail for the one illegal thing he didn't do. He hated Dad, my family, that much."

Becca shivered in the muggy night air. Jared's voice was too calm, too modulated and the laugh that followed his words too harsh.

"No." She held out her hand, not knowing if he'd take

it. Relief and strength filled her when he did and gently stroked the top of her hand with his thumb. "I talked with him. The Sheriff didn't know until the week before Bert died, although he suspected shortly after your father got out of jail when Bert wrote a will leaving his property to Debbie. The Sheriff said Bert had made an offhand comment that had made him feel Bert named Debbie as his heir because he'd thought the Sheriff knew he was driving and had kept his mouth shut. Bert told him about the letter and what he was putting in it."

"The Sheriff's reference to blood money makes sense now. He knew that Bert had made his bequests to us to try and compensate for what he'd done to Dad." Jared pulled his hand from hers and threw himself off the lounge to pace the deck. He stopped next to her chair, loomed over her. "You talked with the Sheriff. What else did he say?"

"Sit down and I'll tell you."

With obvious reluctance he did, tapping the arm of the chair closest to her with his fingers.

Becca recapped her confrontation with the Sheriff.

"The Sheriff and my mother," he said when she finished. "I can't fault him for hating my father for the way he treated Mom. I did for a long time, too, until a pit pastor led me back to my faith."

Becca released her pent-up breath.

"You trust the Sheriff, that he'll get Matt to drop the Family Court petition, and you're okay letting Ari and Brendon visit him and Debbie in Florida?" His eyes narrowed. "He's not forcing you to sign an agreement in exchange for making the Family Court petition go away?"

"No. It was my idea. I'm more comfortable with Brendon and Ari being with their grandparents than with their father, and they like spending time with Ken and Debbie. After we talked, I prayed long and hard for the strength to forgive the Sheriff for what he's done to my family and your family, and I found it in the knowledge that he has to live with what he's done. I also prayed that he and you would be able to have the peace I've found in forgiveness. Can you forgive him?"

A muscle worked in his jaw. "I have to or it will eat at me, affect our lives forever. But he can't move out of Paradox Lake too quickly for me."

Becca laughed, breaking the tension.

Jared rose and offered her his hands. She let him pull her to her feet. For a silent moment, she looked at him framed by the night sky. A sense of rightness that she'd never felt before cloaked her. "I love you," she whispered.

He looked down at her without saying anything, making Becca wonder if she'd spoken those words or only thought them.

Jared cleared his throat. "I know it's too soon to ask you to marry me, but this is fair warning that that's my plan."

She squeezed his hand. "And this is my fair warning that I love you with all of my heart and that I'll be expecting that offer."

A goofy grin spread across his face before his eyes and features grew soft. She tilted up her face and received what she wanted, a toe-curling kiss that sealed the promise of their future.

Epilogue

The following July

"We should have waited and taken our honeymoon after the opening. The ribbon cutting is in fifteen minutes."

"We'll be fine if I drive right to the track." Jared wasn't about to remind Becca that she was the one who'd set their wedding date and had chosen their Alaskan honeymoon cruise. As an old married man of ten days, he knew better than that.

"At least the weather is cooperating today." She glanced out the side window at the clear blue sky. "If it hadn't been thunderstorming in Chicago, we would have been home yesterday. I should have factored in the possibility of weather delays and not booked the extra day in Vancouver after the cruise."

Jared turned on to the newly constructed road to the Sinclair-Miller Motocross Racing School and Track, named for his mentor and Bert Miller. He smiled to himself. You'd think it was her baby, not his—and in a way it was. Without Becca, he never would have realized his dream, any of his dreams, including the ones he hadn't known he had. He reached over and rested his hand on her leg.

"I have it on good authority that they won't start until we get there. I texted Connor from the Albany airport. He said Emily and Drew will have Ari and Brendon at the track so we don't have to stop for them, and Josh is picking up Hope from Grandma's and bringing her along with Gram and Harry."

"You had all that information and you let me fret on like that?"

"Yeah, I was enjoying your enthusiasm for the school. It's kind of cute."

"Humph." She crossed her arms.

"And for the record, as much as the racing school means to me, I wouldn't have given up a minute of our trip to be here sooner."

"Me, either," Becca said.

"Grab my cell and let Connor know we're here."

Jared parked the truck in reserved parking and waited while Becca ran a comb through her hair and checked her makeup she'd freshened at the airport.

"You're beautiful," he said, leaning over and giving her a quick peck. He'd never tire of having her beside him in every way. "Now, we'd better get in." He opened the truck door for her, grabbed her hand and headed for the admissions gate, not realizing his longer stride was making her trot to keep up with him.

"Stop," she said when they breezed through the gate with a wave to people selling tickets. "Let me catch my breath before we go out to the track for the ribbon cutting."

He rolled on the balls of his feet while she took a couple of breaths.

"Who's the one who's excited now?" she asked.

He stilled his restless movement and made a point to shorten his stride as much as he could for the walk to the announcement stand adjacent to the course.

"And here's the man of the hour." Connor spoke into the public announcement system as Jared climbed the steps to the stand.

Jared accepted the microphone from his brother and, with eyes only for Becca waiting by the blue ribbon strung across the start of the course, he welcomed the crowd. As the cheers wound down, he wrapped up with, "Here's Pastor Connor with a benediction before we cut the ribbon and officially open the Sinclair-Miller Motocross Racing School and Track."

He tossed the microphone to Connor and raced down the steps to join Becca and Ari and Hope for the benediction. Behind him, Josh supervised Brendon and his friend Ian, who sat on matching school motocross bikes, engines idling, ready for their inaugural circle of the track.

"Dear Lord," Connor began. "Thank You for giving us such a beautiful day for opening the Sinclair-Miller Motocross Racing School and Track. Bless the track and our youth program services that they will glorify You and lead those who need You to Your way. In Jesus' name, Amen."

His brother signaled Jared, and he and Hope picked up one handle of a pair of comically over-sized scissors while Becca and Ari picked up the other. They snipped the ribbon, and Brendon and Ian took off across the line slowly and carefully as he'd taught them. Jared slipped his arm around Becca's waist and she around his, their other arms circling the girls' shoulders. Together, they watched the boys drive the modified, no-jump course.

Later, he and some of his friends from the circuit would demonstrate some of their racing moves, followed by a race with riders from throughout the region. But for now, it was Jared and Becca and the family he'd never imagined he'd be blessed with. Truly a day of answered prayers.

* * * * *

Dear Reader,

I'm very excited to be returning to Paradox Lake to introduce you to the three Donnelly brothers, starting with Jared, the oldest. Growing up in a small town with a notorious alcoholic father was hard. Not surprisingly, the brothers all left town after high school. But now they're back.

I had fun writing about my reformed "bad boy" Jared, a retired international motocross champion, and the havoc his return to Paradox Lake wreaks on high school history teacher, Becca Norton's life. In my research about motocross, I discovered the Team Faith Ministry (TeamFaith. com). I used their mission—to lead extreme sports athletes to Christ and disciple them so that they will, in turn, lead others involved in or interested in the sport to Christ—as part of Jared's motivation for building his racing school.

I hope you enjoy the fireworks that ensue as Jared wrestles with pursuing his mission and Becca with wanting to do what's best for her family and her community.

Thanks so much for choosing *Winning the Teacher's Heart*. Please feel free to email me at *JeanCGordon@ yahoo.com* or snail mail me at PO Box 113, Selkirk, NY 12158. You can also visit me at Facebook.com/ JeanCGordon.author or JeanCGordon.com or Tweet me at @JeanCGordon.

Blessings,
Jean C. Gordon

REQUEST YOUR FREE BOOKS!

2 FREE INSPIRATIONAL NOVELS
PLUS 2
FREE
MYSTERY GIFTS

Love Inspired®

LI15

Can a widow and widower ever leave their grief in the past and forge a new future—and a family—together?

Read on for a sneak preview of
THE AMISH WIDOW'S SECRET.

"Wait, before you go. I have an important question to ask you."

Sarah nodded her head and sat back down.

"I stayed up until late last night, thinking about your situation and mine. I prayed, and *Gott* kept pushing this thought at me." He took a deep breath. "I wonder, would you consider becoming my *frau*?"

Sarah held up her hand, as if to stop his words. "I…"

"Before you speak, let me explain." Mose took another deep breath. "I know you still love Joseph, just as I still love my Greta. But I have *kinder* who need a mother to guide and love them. Now that Joseph's gone and the farm's being sold, you need a place to call home, people who care about you, a family. We can join forces and help each other." He saw a panicked expression forming in her eyes. "It would only be a marriage of convenience. The girls need a loving mother and you've already proven you can be that. What do you say, Sarah Nolt? Will you be my wife?"

Sarah sat silent, her face turned away. She looked into Mose's eyes. "You'd do this for me? But…you don't know me."

"I'd do this for us," Mose corrected, and smiled.

The tips of Sarah's fingers nervously pleated and un-pleated a scrap of her skirt. "But we hardly know each other. What would people think? They will say I took advantage of your good nature."

Mose smiled. "So, let them talk. They'd be wrong and we'd know it. I want this marriage for both of us, for the *kinder*. We can't let others decide what is best for our lives. I believe this marriage is *Gott*'s plan for us."

Sarah's face cleared and she seemed to come to a decision. She smoothed out the fabric of her skirt and tidied her hair, then finally took Mose's outstretched hand with a smile. "You're right. This is our life. I accept your proposal, Mose Fisher. I will be your *frau* and your *kinder*'s mother."

Don't miss
THE AMISH WIDOW'S SECRET
by Cheryl Williford,
available June 2015 wherever
Love Inspired® books and ebooks are sold.